Between You & Me

Between You & Me

SIKHA BHATTACHARYA

PARTRIDGE
A Penguin Random House Company

Copyright © 2016 by Sikha Bhattacharya.

ISBN: Softcover   978-1-4828-6774-9
       eBook   978-1-4828-6773-2

All rights reserved. No part of this book may be used or reproduced by any means, graphic, electronic, or mechanical, including photocopying, recording, taping or by any information storage retrieval system without the written permission of the author except in the case of brief quotations embodied in critical articles and reviews.

Because of the dynamic nature of the Internet, any web addresses or links contained in this book may have changed since publication and may no longer be valid. The views expressed in this work are solely those of the author and do not necessarily reflect the views of the publisher, and the publisher hereby disclaims any responsibility for them.

Print information available on the last page.

To order additional copies of this book, contact
Partridge India
000 800 10062 62
orders.india@partridgepublishing.com

www.partridgepublishing.com/india

Contents

Author's note ix
Meet Latha.. 1
Where is the Difference? 11
It is a Small World...15
Always a Teacher.. 27
The King of Fruits 31
What's in a Name 34
Blessing in Disguise... 39
The Award 53
MNC.. 59
You cannot forget Preeti... 62
Final Decision 65
Mummy Sunny Samvad.. 80
Return of Ipshita..91
Two Women in My Life 108
Workshop!!!..113
To See or Not To See 117
Life's Small Memories 124

This book is dedicated to my husband Asim, who stood by my all eccentricities, my son Argho and my daughter Shilpi, who think their mum is *bestest*.

Author's note

Everyday so many people come our way.

During work, while shopping, buying vegetables, at the bus stop or taking a walk. We don't talk to them, but somewhere something strikes a chord. You notice their dress or the way they walk or the Mp3 chord stuck to their ears, that lovely complexion or bald head. It can be anything.

You remember people, characters, their characteristics from the village you belong, the school you studied, the college you graduated, from among your friends, place of work...from your neighbourhood.

Some keep frequenting your memories and thoughts. That is when you want to bring them alive...I did that in this book.

The stories are a combination of reality and fiction.

Meet Latha

Year –1982

Place – Madras (Not Chennai then)

Venue –Stella Maris college, 2nd floor, 2nd room to the left of the staircase

People –1st year M.Sc Maths class.

Graduation over, Now into our post graduation, same college, we all, 18 of us were ecstatic. To be back to familiar grounds, known faces, surroundings, lecturers has its own advantages. Another six would be in the class from other colleges.

Stella Maris, the hep and happening college, where there was a lot of brains (that was the impression those days) and a good amount of beauty. We thought of ourselves as a class apart. And why not? Most of us had a good percentage to boast about, walked and talked smart, were sincere in our work, managed good results.

The first day of the class was as usual noisy and chaotic. Meeting each other after two months. All the Hi's! and hellos. The hugs. Everybody wanted to talk at the same time. For us, the old ones, it was old times like before. The new girls looked a little lost, clustered together and found feet in each others company. We, the old ones introduced ourselves, got to know their names, the colleges they came from and made them feel as 'at college 'as possible.

Latha was one of the new ones. Immediately that attracted our attention was her dressing. While we flaunted our pants and tops and strutted around in the latest fashions, here she was all wrapped up in a sari and blouse. Not the trendy sari and blouse which would not have raised our brows, but, sari and blouse more appropriate for rural Tamil Nadu than the college she was in. There was the long well oiled thick jet black plait adorned by jasmine. The red' pottu' (bindi) underlined by 'bibhuti' (incense ash). (There is an incident to share about bibhuti, but later in the following pages). But first impression need not be always the last impression. It happened with Latha. In due course of time, very soon, we more than understood that there was much more to Latha than her ordinary looks and even more ordinary attire.

Six weeks of college and she was by then quite the nucleus of the class. Three things that drew us to her was her intelligence, her way of looking at things differently and her sense of humor, which she often showed by keeping a straight face herself.

Rain or storm, sorry! I am talking about Madras, heat or heat wave, Latha would be occupying her chair in the class unfailingly. We hostelites would remain absent at the slightest pretext. But Monday to Saturday Latha would travel the distance between Guindy and Cathedral road ritually. And better, for who would solve our doubts if she was absent. If she was regular we were relieved. Our life was that much easy. That much was Latha's demand. Supply of her services was also unselfish and unlimited. In short Latha became the apple of all our eyes.

When Latha was present lecturers felt it worthwhile to take the class. When she asked her doubts lecturers got charged. When she disagreed to a particular explanation lecturers took it as a challenge. So we all revolved around Latha the 'sun' of our class. But nobody grudged her the position. We all agreed full heartedly she deserved it.

WE: "six months over start wearing pants", when we saw the expression on her face we immediately changed to, "at least salwars".

LATHA: "Shut up!.All of you will be happily married and enjoying and me? If I walk into my lane dressed like you all, my parents will never find a groom for me. You all want me to live and die a spinster? Not me, not me".

Truly serious problem. Never mind. We liked Latha as she was.

"But your blouses? Your lane has problems if you wear nice fitting blouses, little tighter?. The back neck little lower?"

"Oh! my ammas, I prefer my type of blouses. Keeps away probing eyes. Three of you happily walk from the hostel. Mary, you and you Saras, you come by car".

We were bent on reforming 'our latha'.

"Latha, the sari can be tied lower? please, why sari so high, as if we are going to have floods".

"Good question. Have you all ever run to catch a bus. Try my style, you will never miss a bus. And, if I ramp walk and then tear my saris, you think my mother will spare me?" Once, we all had gone to Golden sands (a beach resort) to enjoy the sun and the sea (of course all covered in jeans and tops) and our Latha invariably in a sari. But thankfully in a nice, bright chiffon. And, what happened. The waves lashed Latha, the chiffon sari like all chiffons shrank by a feet and a half. we were aghast. But latha as unperturbed, prompt came the reply, "saw girls, it is destined my saris should be high up".We all gasped at the reply and the next minute we were rolling with laughter.

Latha had funny answers to all questions. She would reply unfazed. She will make you believe that was the biggest truth. Any way we all loved and enjoyed her crazy reasons.

Latha had big feet. She told us she was fed up of searching for dainty slippers of her size. So what was the solution? She happily used gent's chappals. "That is also protection and this also protects your feet. Should you not be looking at people's faces rather than their feet?" She asked us. Done. We all nodded our approval.

Please do not think she was bossy. That she was leading us by the nose. Far from it. She was a character like this. Jolly. Impish.

We hostelites specialized in eating other's "dabbas's". But we got fed up of Latha's dabba. Square tiffin, filled with white curd rice with a blob of red lime pickle in the centre –we knew it, still we would open it and then make a face.

"It will not change dearies. Early morning that is the only thing I can make. Cannot make mother breathless for my sake, can I? That would be mean. At age 20, I do not want my Amma to run behind me". She reinforced that we need to do things for ourselves. After that, I won't say we loved her curd rice but yes we had the curd rice without making a face.

End of 1st year, she invited us home for a sumptuous, delicious lunch. When we entered, flavours of authentic south Indian cooking tickled our nostrils. And there was the curd rice. She insisted we have it as it was made by her mother. We did, and till day that is one of the best curd rice that I have had. We looked at her mother, she talked to us and we knew, from where Latha had inherited those twinkling eyes and sweet and sour remarks. In those days and times Latha showed us (when we were in her house) how obedient, respectful, she was to her parent and house. Her acceptance of everything in her house was total.

Latha: "where to? Canteen? Stop! Stop! They have flying saucers today". Latha called the hard, dry, round chapattis flying saucers. One day she also calculated the distance it will travel if thrown at a given speed, taking its mass and weight into consideration. Crazy girl with crazier friends around her. Life was fun.

At the canteen table --Latha: "Hey Babu, (our canteen boy) water in the Red hill reservoir has increased or what?" if the sambar was watery - that was the comment that came from her. Surprisingly Babu came out with a weak, "Akka enna Akka ni cholre ".Translated, it means 'elder sister what are you saying'.

I should not forget this incidence under any circumstance. Madras IIT used to have (may be having them still) their annual fest 'Mardi Gras'. Stella Marians were invited. Sister Principal would receive the invite and we (only the senior students) were given permission to go. During the different events, friendship's developed, romances bloomed and we came to know, later many culminated into marriages too. We all would be joking, laughing passing comments.

Someone will say "Samira, that one is for you", pointing to a boy with porcupine hair. Samira under her breath, "Kill you all. find someone better".

Saras would be all open mouthed "look so handsome!!"

"May be full of his looks, therefore boring" retorted Laila.

"Look, Look, Look! all suited, booted. Has he come for a fest or a reception? Not for me. You all can have him"

Such bantering continued. Then our Latha, "Girls you all are wasting time. I have finalized my choice".

We: "Latha you 'choopa rustom 'where? where? Which one? One to the left?" We knew it will be a laughing bomb, but we were still curious. We ourselves were trying to locate the guy of Latha's interest. "There he is, wearing a red pottu like me with white bibhuti below. Matching 'matching'. What say you all?" We all burst out ignoring the sniggering look around us. That was latha lovably unpredictable.

God has this in him. when you want the days to fly, it will linger and linger on. When you want the calendar page to remain stuck, you will find there is a fast forward. Months will come and go before you bat an eye lid. Our second year of post graduation was like 'this….' Fun, studies, sorry! the other way round, studies, fun and viola the exam was literally round the corner.

We all planned an evening out. Happy and sad at the same time. From our limited allowances, we chose our gifts. Finally we were all standing outside Blue Diamond for a movie and later dinner at Southern Chinese. We all had packets in our hands. We could all make out the little gifts in each other's packets for each other. But, our Latha, a small clutch purse –that is all. We confined our surprise to ourselves. Knowing Latha, anything can happen any time. Nothing is impossible.

At the restaurant we decided to give those little tokens of love and togetherness which will bring back fond memories. Then came the most touching gift ---right out of latha's clutch purse, Small 4" by 4" sandalwood pieces (thickness of card board), on it was written 'the fragrance will remain forever so will the fragrance of our friendship'. Simple, sweet and it said it all. What better way to convey your deepest feelings. All of us were floored. In our hearts we agreed so much to learn from Latha.

Exams over. Results were out. Goes without saying, Latha topped. Initially regular letters, then their frequency like all other things reduced. Wedding cards came, we were all settling down to a new life of job, marriage and eventually kids. Now and then news of others floated in. Someone had a baby, so and so left for the states, one of us got a promotion. Life took its natural course. We were all settled in our little worlds of family and job.

So many years passed. Twenty years. Yes, that was twenty years back.

I was working with a nationalized bank and they sent me to Banaras on an official visit. Day's work done, I was walking up 'Vishwanath gali' for my darshan. There in front of me was a very very familiar (still) black plait with jasmine. The sari (not so high) but still high compared to other sari clad ladies around. The gait –same old brisk walk. Before I knew, I called out 'Latha', before I realized, the lady turned around and the next moment we were in each other's arms. We were laughing, crying and talking at the same time. Shops around knew what a re-union is. Any way, who cares, this was an unbelievable bonanza. We finished our darshan quickly (even Kashi Vishwanath forgave us the hurry).We settled with Kachodis, rabdi and lassi and, and those were the days (hours and minutes) my friend we thought should never end. (excuse me the aberration).

She had come to immerse her mother's ashes in the Ganges. That was aunty's wish. I saddened at the recollection of those twinkling eyes and the twinkling diamonds on her right nostril. Latha broke my reverie. "come on don't feel sad for ma, she won't like it, where ever she is. Instead remember her curd rice and all her blessings will be yours"

"Latha you have not changed. Age, marriage, job, children, you are still the same".

"If I changed, you wouldn't be sitting and talking to me, you would have pushed me into the Ganges. If I change now and go home, hubby and children will look at me as if I am an alien and the little one will ask "amma, ennachi amma?" (ma what happened ma). Don't you think changing is too much of a risk!.

"yeah, be as you were, the day you change you will lose a friend".

Suddenly, "look at this", she had taken out her feet from under the table and dainty lovely sandals adorned her feet. "see the change".

"Why? What happened to your gents chappals?"

"Yaar, mine and hubby's chappals were all getting mixed. Worse, 'the broken chappals were all mine' he said. So now I put him in his place".

Laughing, I choked over my rabdi. We laughed, we talked, we shared, we exchanged news of all our friends, classmates. We were trying to squeeze everything out of the ticking hands of our watches.

Time and tide wait for none. Taught in the second grade, how, how true, realized it at the age of forty two in Benares, when we stood up to part. Then, "Latha you never told me or I did not ask, what are you doing?"

"Teaching, Sikha"

"Wow! which college? Under grads or post grads?"

"In school".

I know disappointment showed large on my face. Our Latha, intelligent, best, always first, teaching in school? I salvaged the situation.

"Oh great! Teaching the senior school, xith and the xiith graders?"

"I teach the 6th, 7th and the 8th graders". Enough. I could not contain myself any more.

"But, why Latha, with all those firsts, medals and certificates".

"Remember the math fear. How people were scared of numerical. How they had a mind set. You say 32 multiplied by 100 and immediately a blank look".

"Sikha this happens, when they did not love the subject but did it because they needed to be promoted to the next class. I want students to enjoy Maths. Play with numbers. have a good grasp, think and enjoy numbers. 'aaj mazaa aaya' should be the reaction. They should have fun learning the subject. Not take it like a bitter pill every day".

"If I teach the xith and the xiith they have already built walls around them. Their prejudices have become concrete. I want to start with them young. When supple, ready to receive and learn with an open mind leading to a ready heart. In the higher classes they will not ask how to find the square root of a five digit number. They will be too shy".

I understood, I followed Latha's thought process. Only she could think like this. While we were all chasing posts, positions, climbing the career ladder, comparing our salaries, counting our increments, here she was, on a different plane altogether, the highest plane. We learnt to earn. She learnt to give. Only she could be like this and she could do things that were very different with full conviction.

We hugged. I held her tightly. We got on to our respective rickshaws. We took different directions. We waved. The distance between the two rickshaws grew. But I was even more close to Latha, even more close. I learnt one more life's lessons from her.

Where is the Difference?

Marjina stood in front of my aunt's critical eye. Disapproval oozed, as her eyes moved from the unkempt, uncombed, brown, oil-less hair to the over sized blue flower printed frock, which repeatedly slipped off from one shoulder as there were no buttons to hold it together, to the thin limbs called hands, that were still sticky from the mango that she had on her way, to the muddy feet. The object of her cynosure was quiet oblivious of the appraisal she was going through, interested more in the children playing in the courtyard. Given the chance, she would have dashed off in a jiffy and joined them.

"Her mother ran away with some man and Gaffur (our farm hand) has no one to look after the children. Anyway, you also needed someone to take care of your small chores, I thought this will solve both Gaffur 's and your problem", my cousin said, as he waited for an answer. My aunt conceded, though not very pleased with the Marjina package, but, where do you get people these days. Thus began the Marjina chapter in our house.

Marjina looked much smaller than her age of twelve. Initially, between work she ran off to play house-house or seven tiles with the other children, much to the chagrin of my aunt, who never missed the opportunity to give her a good dressing down. That she belonged to a different religion was prime on my aunt's mind. But who cared! Marjina enjoyed it all—the work, the running away, playing and finally the scolding. She would often retort in her childish way, "What a Granny! Never happy" or in a very wise tone "These old people are all the same". "Now tell me quickly what I should do, they are all waiting for me to play, then, don't shout".

Everybody, the men, women and the children accepted Marjina as a part of the family. Another child, another member to be loved and looked after like the rest. So much so, Marjina now stopped going home and found bed and bedding in our house, but where? On the floor of my aunts room, next to her bed. Even after more than a year of her stay, my aunt was still skeptical and allowed her entry into her room (with reservation). With a sigh, she now commented, "Let her be, she is handy when I want water or go to the toilet at night". Nobody knew then, it would be few years before she would graduate to my aunt's bed itself.

The next few years the house reverberated with, "Marjina didi, I can't find my uniform", "Marjina, where are you?, grind the masala fast, your brother needs to leave for office early", "Marjina did you see my umbrella?". Marjina, Marjina, Marjina, no other person was so much in demand. In the meantime Marjina had grown older, now in her late teens, filled out with food, love and security and grown authoritative too. "You bappa, I will slap you if you throw your things around". "Mejo boudi (majhli bhabi), you have left money on the table again, so careless!". "Today's fish curry is delicious. Cook with mustard paste always."

My aunt? The picture had reversed. Now Marjina ordered and aunt obeyed meekly. "Granny enough of puja, it is already late for your breakfast, did your God tell that you have to pray on an empty stomach?"

"Okay" my aunt conceded "My years of practice, I have to give it up for you. What did your Allah say about your praying?"

"Oh! My Allah said, have a good breakfast and look after granny." And they burst out laughing together.

My aunt became totally dependent on Marjina. Marjina was the maid, the help, the doctor, the adviser, the treasurer, the gossip supplier and the DAUGHTER.

Life continued. It was time to get our daughter married. My cousins rejected several offers. "That boy is no good, always wiling away his time with a bidi in his mouth". "No, No, the family is too large. Poor girl will be up to her neck with work the whole day". "The boy is from too far a village, getting her will be a problem". My bhabis wanted a fellow with a 'government job' ---at least there will be a secure income.

Finally we found all the desirable qualities of good character, good family, good government job in Arif, and Marjina was married off with a cycle and a wrist watch for her groom. My different cousins contributed and Marjina started off with more or less everything that a new house hold needs, plus a bonus of small gold ear studs and a thin chain --- yes courtesy my aunt. The whole house hold cried. Some openly, some secretly. Marjina had started crying a week before the wedding. My aunt remained in bed, turned to the wall for a week.

Life normalized, but it was not the same. There was a lacuna. Children seemed dull, elders looked lost, my aunt was paralyzed without Marjina. When she came back for the first time, it was as if it was Durga puja. Noise, laughter, fish of Marjina's choice and what not.

Marjina was called for every occasion. "The marriage is on the 14th, write a post card to Marjina, 'she should be here by the 5th'. Who will take care of everything?" Still every thing revolved round the absent Marjina. Like the daughter, she came and went, joy when she came and sadness when she left.

My aunt fell sick. Only name she had on her lips was Marjina, her eyes staring at the door for that familiar figure to come in. Marjina arrived and took over. Slept by her side, nursed her by the night, cleaned her by the day. She herself forgot to eat, rest, sleep. She read the Quran sitting by her side. Amidst the reading of the Quran and the Gita, my aunt breathed her last. Marjina cried the loudest and the longest.

That was ten years back. Today, Marjina is a portly woman with two children, with whom she fondly shares her growing up in this house. Her eyes turn misty when she recalls granny. She is still a part and parcel of the household, every happening, every function.

Either way we cannot think of each other without each other. So I ask a question, WHO IS A MUSLIM? WHO IS A HINDU? We are all one, all together. As individuals we feel for each other. we care for each other, we laugh and cry together.

THEN WHY THIS DIFFERENTIATION? IS IT THAT- WE ARE GOOD AS INDIVIDUALS BUT FAIL AS A COMMUNITY?

It is a Small World

I reached CST station at 4.45 pm. Another forty minutes to go before they gave the train on the platform. I looked at the AC waiting room at a distance, then decided against it. All the way up and within minutes once again all the way down. Not worth the trouble. That is the time I decided to indulge in my favorite past time. watching people. The hustle –bustle of a station, the hurrying crowd, fit of activity, movement attracted me. Most of all the anonimity in a station was what attracted me most. My anonimity. Nobody looked at me. Nobody bothered why I was sitting in one of the steel chairs. Nobody wanted to know why I was at the CST. Why I was travelling out. whether I was alone or they did not look around for my family. Nobody stopped for a moment to look at my neck, my ears, and part of my forehead. This always happened. They looked, whether old acquaintances or an unknown person. Their eyes did travel across my forehead, to my ears and turn to my neck. More inquisitive people sometimes surreptiously looked at my arms and hands too. Well, forget it. I am too used to all that now. Yes, initially it was embarrassing. later irritating, when I saw looks of pity cross their face. But now I have this Couldn't –care –less attitude or ignore.

So I sat there. Most of the time enjoying the sights, sometimes puzzled, sometimes just a plain observer watching a slide show of people, things, scenes. Why do mothers always have to drag children? Why is it some people have to have so much of luggage? You will see the same man running up and down the length of the station once, twice, thrice and you will wonder whether to laugh or cry at his condition. The tea stall fellow is a 'Dasha bhuja' (Goddess Durga with ten hands) Giving tea, samosa, juice, counting money, giving instructions, answering passing people's enquiries. Time passed and my train chugged in.

So nice to get into an AC coach. After the heat and dust of the platform, the calm and cool of the compartment seem heaven sent. I settled by the window. Co-passengers trickled in. I kept count. One more passenger to go. I felt the other passengers scrutiny on me. Again the side wise glance at my forehead, ears, neck. It is going to be my life time company then why do I have this feeling of unease and sudden bitterness. Some things you cannot help. You cannot go tie a handkerchief on people's eyes. I looked out of the window. Minutes ticked by. The discomfort within me settled. I was once again composed internally and got back to general looking around, thinking about the meeting in Mumbai, office in Delhi, my home where I lived alone.

The last passenger came in. I was shocked. I immediately looked around to make sure no one saw my expression. What I had on my forehead, ears and neck, she had it all over. We both have leukoderma. It is not dangerous, it is not contagious, it doesn't throw doubts on your character, it is not life taking, still why is it such a taboo? Why are we treated differently? People act normal but they are not normal with us. That little distance between body and heart, people will maintain. That small chasm will remain, hard to be bridged. Neither a foot will come forward nor a hand will beckon you to be close. Slowly, but firmly we manage to carry on.

Her luggage had a name tag. Shiuli Chatterjee. Shiuli, that lovely, fragrant flower, white petals with orange stem. Chatterjee, touched a distant, chord. That was my married surname. I was Chatterjee once. I was married to Sitanshu Chatterjee. I was known as Mrs. Chiroshree Chatterjee. A Bengali girl with a fair share of good looks, good complexion, long thick black hair, on the taller side accompanied by a good figure. I got compliments for my expressive eyes and a charming smile which showed even white teeth. So my father had named me 'Chiroshree'. Chiro meaning 'always' and shree meaning 'charming'.

The train speeded. Out side the passing scenario speeded, with it speeded my thoughts. School, college and then suddenly halted –my marriage. 'Shiuli Chatterjee' with leukoderma like me, a surname that once was mine, brought back hordes of memory. Thoughts which I had pushed to the farthest corner of my mind and piled over it my new life, suddenly pushed its way up and stared at me, forcing me to think on this idle day, by a train window.

A typical Bengali drawing room with typical Bengali elders looked down on Chiroshree and Sitanshu hoping that the boy-seeing- girl will end on a positive note. When Chiroshree looked at five feet eight inches tall Sitanshu with thick black hair and an equally thick black moustache, sharp intelligent eyes and an athletic body. She knew her answer would be 'yes'. Her sixth sense told her, his answer would also be 'yes'. Their qualifications, job, aspirations, college, family back ground had already gone through microscopic surveillance. So this was final.

With the sound of shehnai behind her, Chiroshree entered her new household in BHEL colony in Tiruchirapally. Sitanshu worked there. Iife was- as everybody dreams of.

Sitanshu was understanding, "Come on don't get up. Sleep some more. I have managed toast and egg for many years during my bachelor days. One more day for my dear wife. He was helpful and sharing. "Here I have donned your apron. Just tell me the inches and the centimeters and I will chop your vegetables".

Endowed with a good sense of humour he would come up with, "Chiro I will cut onions for you".

"Why onions out of all vegetables?"

"Because when I cry chopping onions, you will hug me and wipe my flowing tears ". Observant, he would notice the minutest details. "Wow! My pretty wife looks even prettier. Wear maroon more often" or "New sheets on the bed? Are we celebrating our monthly anniversary?"

They would zoom off on their Yezdi, the very fashionable bike those days outside city limits to walk hand in hand and feel the cool village breeze on their faces.

"Get in, get in, it is raining".

"Chiro you come out, let us get wet. I have never seen a rain drenched lady except in Hindi movies".

Life was too beautiful and it continued like that for three years, seven months and twelve days.

As usual Chiro was in front of the dressing table tying up her hair high for the night. Hair on the neck at night irritated her.

"What is it behind your ear?"

"Behind my ear?" Chiro moved her fingers behind her right ear, brought it in front of her eyes, there was nothing. "There is nothing".

"No there is some thing", he was watching her from the bed. He got up, came and stood behind her, looked and said, "there is a white spot, the size of a coin".

Chiro had not noticed it, being right behind her year. He brought a small mirror behind her. She could now see it in the reflection. Her heart sank. But why? It can be any skin distortion, then why this sinking feeling.

"Don't worry, don't look as if catastrophe has struck. we will go to a skin specialist and it will be fine. Some ointment, some tablets and it will vanish like this". He clicked his fingers. "Daag dhundte raha jaoge".

Worst fears came true. Questions came flooding to her 'Why me?'. 'What have I done God to deserve this?'. 'Will it be the same between her and Sitanshu?' 'Just as it is now?' 'How will others react to the news?' Her father. Her Mother. She could'nt think any more. She did not remember any body, far and wide in her family having it. Where did she get it from?.

She brooded-- day and night 'In her waking hours, in her sleep, while stirring the subzi in the kadahi, while watering her plants'. Unconciously her hands would move behind her years, unknowingly she would walk down to the mirror and peer behind her ears folding it till painful. It was always there sitting tight knowing nothing could dislodge it.

The doctor confirmed, it was leukoderma. Some one had opened a tap of frozen water on her heart. She could hear the Doctor's voice from a distant assuring her, giving her confidence, telling her how medicines help in containing the spread etc. etc. etc.... But, she felt lost, absolutely lost.

She felt defeated. She felt helpless. Days and months that followed, she came to terms with it, but all the time the feeling as if she had failed Sitanshu, remained. It can happen to anyone and nobody wishes for it. Then why the feeling of loneliness laced with guilt. Sitanshu soothed and comforted her. Life went on. But it was not the same. Something was missing. Those conservations, loving, sometimes meaningless, sometimes fun, those running into each others arms, those reaching out for each other in bed was slowly but distinctly reducing. Chiro wondered 'will life be the same ever again? Is she the same?'. No. Then how can everything be the same.

She often observed Sitanshu keenly without his knowing. To notice that little difference in behaviour, if any. Fortunately it was not there.

But her relief was short lived. As the patch spread, peeping from behind her ears it spread to her chin and neck, there were spots on both her elbows and knuckles. She knew very soon it would possess her here, there and everywhere. May be Sitanshu was also thinking on the same lines. He would now immerse himself behind the news paper with his cup of tea. Chiro remembered the unread newspapers before, which they would look at and laugh while stacking. Chiro also found it hard to find conservation. She would move to the kitchen, but he would not follow. The distance grew and so did the distance between them in bed. It was more than a year now, neither the leukoderma nor the relationship was improving.

The train stopped. I was jolted back to the present. Already Nagpur. I didn' t even know we had covered this much of distance. So immersed I was in my Chiroshree – Sitanshu flash back.

Ditch! Ditch! Ditch. That was ten years back and why am I sitting in the cool comfort of a confirmed second AC seat and suffering the heat by digging up the past. But

Shiuli Chatterjee my front seat co –passenger, her surname triggered it all off.

She, Shiuli smiled at me. A friendly and warm smile. May be she felt close to me, we suffered the same fate. Oh! how cynical I had become. I smiled back. I decided to be civil and strike a conservation. A better option than looking out blindly at the passing lush fields, quaint huts, shady trees, local people and going back to the Chiroshree – Sitanshu movie, that too a tragic one.

Shiuli and I seemed to click. She was Kolkata based, born and brought up there, married for the past six years, no kids, worked as a teacher. She had come to Mumbai for a teacher's meet of her subject. I shared my bit too. Like her a thorough Calcacian, married once, now a single determined woman working with one of the multinationals, had come to Mumbai for a meeting, which, I announced gladly and may be smiling widely (first time after I got into the train) went on well to my satisfaction.

"You were married, what happened? Sorry! I should'nt have asked. It just spilled out".

"It's Okay, we divorced, that was many years back. It doesn't hurt to talk about it anymore".

"Sorry again, don't think of me as rude, but is it because of these marks? I ask you because we both have this in common".

"Yes, we were drifting apart. The spontaneity in our marriage was missing. There was some unnamed reservation between us. We were together and we were far apart".

"Then?"

"I found he was not comfortable either at home or outside with a wife having leukoderma patches. I loved him Shiuli. I did not want to imprison him for life. I did'nt want to see myself as an unwanted baggage to be shouldered for life".

"How did it finally happen?"

"It was not easy. The first day I broached the topic, I still don't know how I had the guts to propose the end of our marriage. But it was not the result of one day thinking or a spur of the moment suggestion. I had spent many days and sleepless nights over it".

"I still remember my husbands shocked face. Things were not congenial, but he never expected anything so drastic". Silence on either side.

"By the way why am I sharing so much with you, a stranger, a person whom I know only for the past eight to ten hours" I asked. Shiuli laughed. A child like innocent laugh laced with some sadness. "You are forgetting we are the birds of the same feather. Tell me the rest and I will tell you why I am eager to know about it".

I continued, "Discussions, arguments, counter arguments continued. It was not easy, but taking all pros and cons, he should be free from an uncomfortable marriage and look forward to a better life minus a wife with spreading leukoderma and I should have the freedom to look forward to a life of self respect minus the guilt of pinning down a person, plus a career for me, a post graduate in Economics should do well. That is all – THE END".

Shiuli kept quiet. I wanted her to say, say something about us, say something about herself. No, She just leaned back and fell silent. I looked at her still hoping her to speak. She looked back at me but she was far away. I let her be. This train journey should not be a collection of sad stories, first mine, then Shiuli's.

But I consoled myself, Shiuli's is a happy story, she and her husband are together. With that satisfying thought I went back to staring out of the window. Human mind, it cannot sit idle, thoughts flitted. Thanks to the chaiwala, for a much needed intervention. Took mine and extended one to Shiuli, she was still lost in her own world of thoughts. She took the tea, then suddenly, "But Chiroshree why does my husband not agree to a divorce? I too want, like you, to relieve himself and me from this burden. But, no. He won't even listen to me".

How lucky! I thought to myself. Here was someone who was holding on to his wife inspite of the disease. Here was someone who wanted to continue the marriage inspite of everything. "It's mad", I said. "He wants the marriage to survive, to last, and here you are hell bent on breaking it".

"He is not happy, neither am I" said Shiuli. "But there is something that I cannot put my fingers on that keeps him from ending the union. I thought over it a million times but I can't find the answer. And very stubbornly he says a big No".

"May be he loves you still, he cannot think of the coming years without you, may be you are not able to fathom his love for you, may be ……..", she stopped me by lifting her finger.

"You think I am not intelligent enough to understand all this which you are trying to put forward so comfortably to me. No Chiroshree there is something, till I find out, the puzzle will remain to torcher me" As an afterthought she added "he looks very sad and dejected though".

"Come let us have another cup of tea and put an end to not very welcome thoughts and conversations".

"Right".She agreed willingly. "We talk of other things".

"You will be going right upto Delhi?"

"Yes" I said. "I live in C.R. Park".

"Ha! You want Kolkata all around you in Delhi too, right?"

"Yes, from ruii maach (Rohu fish) to egg roll you get it all. By the way you too till Delhi?".

"No Bhopal. Hubby works with BHEL".

BHEL? All the newly started good conversation blew out of my head, once again old thoughts rushed to take the empty space. Sitanshu was also in BHEL Trichi. Too many coincidences with Shiuli. First the surname and now BHEL. I brushed aside all such thoughts. Is Chatterjee an uncommon name? Of course not. Every third Bengali is a Chatterjee. And other people can't work in BHEL or not?

Time flew. Shiuli and Chiroshree looked at each other, dived back into their own world ---similar world. Silence followed conversation and conversation followed silence. Another twenty, twenty five minutes and this new found friend 'like –me' would alight and be gone. Should I take her address. Her mobile number at least. Later, just before she gets down, she has just closed her eyes.

As the train slowly entered, Shiuli got ready with her luggage, a stroller. We stood up, looked at each other, hugged and held each others arm. I spoke first, "See shiuli, when the marriage is on, he wants to continue, you don't become hyper and put a spanner in the works. Don't imagine reasons and put an unwanted, untimely end to something so important called 'your marriage'. Right? You will remember?"

She gave a nod. "Come down. Meet my husband. He will be there at the station to receive me."

We alighted. We waited in the crowd. A tall man with thick black hair and equally thick black moustache walked briskly towards us. Sitanshu here, after so many years, in Bhopal station, walking towards me. I was stunned. I felt my face flush, beads of perspiration appeared on my face and neck. My chest was constricted. I wanted to turn around and rush into the compartment. I couldn't. I was with Shiuli, yet to meet her husband.

"Chiroshree" Shiuli said "Meet my husband Sitanshu". She continued, "Sitanshu, we became friends. Meet Chiroshree. She is going to Delhi, works there".

Then, "Are you okay Chiro?, (She had to call like Sitanshu also, at the last moment). Why sweating so much? Some water? Sure you are fine?"

"I Think it is the heat. Specially after the AC coach. I am okay". I looked at Sitanshu. "Hello", my voice sounded inebriated, weak.

"Hello" he said, discomfort written all over his face. There was silence. Some lose talk, which entered neither my ears nor my head. Only one thing was buzzing in my head, Sitanshu after all these years, out of all places, me standing on Bhopal platform in front of Sitanshu because of a train acquaintance called Shiuli.

True, this world is full of surprises. "You get inside, you are sweating too much".

"Yeah, bye then". I exchanged no address, no mobile number. I boarded the train, a last glance showed me both walking towards the exit. Did I notice a droop to his shoulders. Imagination, I told myself.

I sat once again by the window. The train was whistling past a raging whirlwind outside. My mind felt no different. It was in turmoil. Questions raced in my mind first to the second to the third ………Will Sitanshu tell her who I was? Will Shiuli know why I looked so unwell all of a sudden in the station? Will Sitanshu wonder if Shiuli knew who her 'few hours' of co passenger was. I had no clue, no answer. There was no mobile number to find out.

One answer I knew and Shiuli didn't know, 'Why Sitanshu refused a divorce so vehemently'. But one answer I didn't have was, Why God let it happen to Sitanshu a second time'.

Always a Teacher

NOBLE PROFESSION. Yes. It is teaching.

Most teachers are reluctant teachers. Somewhere along the line that coveted, desirable career became out of reach. Average marks, family responsibilities, financial constraints, different reasons come in the way & one is forced to turn to the teaching profession. I say so with some conviction (I can't vouch for it) & very teacherishly support with statistical data. One regular question on the last day of my class "So, how many of you will take up teaching?" No hands up, most of the time. They all look at each other & smile apologetically. In their mind the thought process is, "Hope she doesn't feel bad. But definitely I don't want to be a teacher", or "Why should I be a teacher, I have been an 80 percenter through out". Another reaction is "When banking, IAS, IFS, UPSC, CA. CS, everything is there to choose then, Why a teacher?" I too was no exception. Of course we have the others. They will swear by teaching. The love for their subject & their love to continue to immerse in their subject & knowing its nuances from every angle makes them take up this worthy profession. Pay, perks & position are far from their mind.

Most teachers are lady teachers. Most comfortable. You learn, you earn & at the same time you look after your hearth & home. Only job that allows you to balance, that too beautifully, your personal with the professional.

Once again, I too was not an exception. Because, when I was doing my post graduation & afterwards when I was a fresh bubbling PG in Economics (that too with Statistics & Mathematical Economics), my head was full of career options like – being an IAS officer. Okay, if not that, then at least an officer in one of the nationalized banks or maybe something to do with researching the field of Economic theory. Today after 30 years I am a teacher.

Regrets? NONE WHAT SO EVER. In fact I cannot think of any other profession—in Economics or any other streams that can be as interesting & have so much of variety & most of all vibrate so much with that very essence called life. Imagine travelling from district to district looking into farmer's problems, pressing a riot, preparing a budget (as an IAS officer) compared to a class full of lively eager faces. Today visualizing my self in an air conditioned office, sitting on a well cushioned chair, pouring over five & ten digit figures, racking my brains over drafts, deposits & dues seem to be very boring when you see bright faces wishing "good morning! ma'am", or worried faces with a doubt in statistics. Those ledgers full of figures will never smile back at me & say "Thanks Ma'am, that was so simple". Instead of delving into what lies in the dead craters of the moon (someone has to do that also) to me, delving into young minds, their likes & dislikes, what makes them tick this moment & what freezes them to zero degrees the next is much more rewarding.

The changes you notice are breath taking. The shortest, shy boy becomes the tallest outgoing boy by the time he is in the XII standard. Oh! so dull Simi of class VII is brimming with ideas after two years. New friendships emerge, old friends split. That damn-a-care Paritosh all of a sudden becomes over conscious of his looks & turn out. Umpteen cases like this. For a teacher the school gate opens to a new vista every day. Every day there is a change to be noticed. Every day she changes herself. Her students make her dynamic, vigilant, up to date & young at heart.

We teach our subjects. We see the interest growing in their eyes, at that moment –we are the best, we are complete. They want to know & we have the answers. We are reflected in their eyes. Then can we afford to be anything other than the best? There is immense satisfaction when we wipe out a rolling tear from an innocent cheek, when we wipe out lines of worry from a young forehead or we just join in merry laughter over a silly joke. Sure, along the years our head & heart are full of these sprightly imps called students.

After a few years their faces fade. They once again come alive when we receive a birthday card, a happy teachers day message or their wedding invite. Or a "Hi ma'am" across a crowded room. Or a nice lift when on a scorching afternoon there is neither a bus or an auto rickshaw in sight. In no profession past moments come alive so vividly.

At the cost of sounding very selfish, let me tell you, teaching has rich dividends. When an important paper fails to move on a beauracratic table, a student of yours will pop up & while you wait in his air conditioned office, your work is done & complete. Your doctor students are a blessing. When you are waiting for your reports & imagining the worst, your doctor student will help you to take the right decision. Somewhere amidst all your worry & tension you know you are in the right hands. Bookings by rail or air, help in an unknown city, receiving you in foreign lands, enquiring about how you are keeping can come only from this profession. With face book & what's up, the connectivity is even greater. They know all about you & you about them.

Of course a gynecologist will say "I take the pleasure of bringing a new life into the world"—I would say "why, that little brat with a puckered up face, waling away to glory, eyes tightly shut doesn't even acknowledge your presence". Pilots would boast of being on cloud nine on their job, what happens if you have a hijacker on board? Engineers –What's so pleasurable with feeling less, Lifeless contraptions of steel.

The best introduction that I had so far was, "Diku you have a ma'am I too have my ma'am, meet my economics Ma'am". I can go on & on -----that is why I am a (good!!!) teacher, but in short what I am getting at is BE A TEACHER ONCE ……YOU WILL REMAIN A TEACHER ALWAYS.

The King of Fruits

Oh! It is almost going, going gone – The mango season of course.

I waited (every year), I ate, I enjoyed the fruit for the last 50 years—and suddenly I realized how, how very wonderful the fruit is, not in the fruity sense alone but in many other ways too.

This is one fruit where, with a plateful of it, you don't have to run over sofas, upstairs, downstairs and play hide and seek. It is the other way round, the children chased me with, "cut out the milk Ma, give me a mango". Am I hearing it right? Scenes of cut, oxidized apples, stale pear, watering papayas flashed in my mind. I only fell short of falling at their feet (please allow me my bit of exaggeration) requesting them to finish those fruits (bought by their father's hard earned money).

This is one fruit which brings the family together. The son is toooo busy, Friends you know. The daughter is busier, Mobile you know. Husband is the busiest. office calls. Office matters you know. But, come the mango season, the scenario is a complete volte face with calls from all corners, "Call me when you have mangoes". Even more surprising, I hold on to the stair case balustrade to keep myself from falling, "Hello everybody, come, I have cut the mangoes"---from my lazy son, who does not lift a finger even to drive a fly off his nose.

Guests too behave differently with mangoes. Its too late for coffee, cannot sleep. No, No, -- No nimbu pani please, I have an acidity problem. But when the yellow, cubed, chilled mango is served, people actually pull their chairs, get as close to the fruit as possible. NO - nos, no - nothings, just attack.

Epics have it that Raja Janak wanted to send something unique in Sita's 'shagun'. The koel said, it would sing and create a fruit that no one ever saw or tasted before. Throughout spring the Koel sang full throated. The mango flowers bloomed, followed by the small mangoes, which took shape of full fledged fruit. The Koel sang on with even more gusto. The summer heat increased, the mangoes caught on the yellow hue, the koel continued with its throatful melody.

It was now weak with days of singing and bogged down by the summer heat. Still, the little bird continued its melodious singing relentlessly. With doubled efforts it waited for the day when Raja Janaks face would be alight with pleasure on seeing this novel fruit solely created for his dear daughter Sita. Little did the little bird know that God deigned it other wise. The Koel fainted out of sheer exhaustion. It was totally oblivious to the fact that during the period of its unconsciousness. The luscious fruit had ripened, reached Ayodhya and enjoyed by one and all. No body remembered the little Koel. Wth the first rains the bird regained consciousness. She looked around for the fruit. Where was it? The bird assumed it had failed. Ashamed by its failure, it just flew away. Till today the Koel is heard while the mango grows and after the mango ripens the 'cooo' just vanishes.

Who is a sycophant? Don't know? The mango season will tell you that there are these particular genre of people who, in the mango season will arrive with a crate of this delicious fruit. They will tell you in many words, how it is no trouble at all, how it is from their very own orchard, and how it is an immense pleasure to gift you these coveted fruits. Then, one day you retire from office, or you are given a different department or you are no more a profitable proposition as you were before. Then, summer may come or summer may go but mangoes will never come. Who is a sycophant? Where is he? Now you know the answer.

Remember your school days? A mango must have been the best drawing that you ever did –easiest to draw and lovely to colour.

There are n number of fabulous things I can recall about mangoes. Even, if you think, you will see, many sides to the shapely fruit and know why it has earned the title of 'The king of fruits'.

What's in a Name

Yes, they named her KARUNA. That is her grandmother & mother. Pushpavalli, Lajwanti, Hemangini, Bhagyalakshmi were the names making the rounds. In that Karuna was novelty personified. Karuna meaning compassion, pity. Little did the child and the reveling crowd around know that the owner of the name would become in the future, a person, who will be followed by looks of pity. But not always. Because she decided to change it, that is the later part of the story.

Born into an affluent family, her father was a British railway employee, a welcome girl child after the first male sibling. At three months when she learnt to smile actually her crying began. She lost her father to a two day fever. While she was snug in her mother's lap, smiled and gurgled and grew, she did not see the tears that flowed down her mother's cheek and the look of pity that was directed towards her.

As if that was not enough, her grandmother, guardian of the whole family signed off from her earthly duties, not being able to bear the loss of her only son.

It was best for them, her mother, her three year old brother and her to move to her maternal uncle. Her uncle and aunt accepted them with some measure of love and some amount of 'duty to be done'. Her mother took over a lot of household duties to be useful and wanted. She was

Between You & Me

left to grow with the other children of the household. She would be often puzzled when visitors, the neighbours, the village people gave her pitying looks. Anyway she was too small to understand these worldly looks.

As she grew up, the meaning of those pitying glances dawned on her. She understood, she was different. She did not have a father. She did not live in her own house. She understood why there were so many 'NOS' for her. The biggest no was 'DON'T ASK'.

An intelligent child, she kept herself busy with her studies and helping her mother. She was extra careful that there was no reason for complain from any quarter.

Then came two situations, when she pitied and pitied herself. She had a fairly melodious voice. The music teacher had a soft corner for her, coupled with pity for the fatherless child. He took interest and taught her. But one day her uncle declared "No more music lessons. I have said no to the music teacher. For marriage you need to cook, keep house, may be embroider and knit. Do that". She pitied herself and accepted the dictum.

The second time she pitied herself and burst out crying, which continued silently for months to come. In Bengal those days in grade IV, there was something called 'Britti Parikkha' or scholarship examination. She stood first and got a scholarship of four annas. For once, instead of pity applause came her way. She was ready for her matric exam. Her village did not have a centre. They had to go to a neighbouring village, Beledanga, now in Bangladesh, for the exam. Boys of the village, all of them, with ration, lantern, kerosene, books, cart load of things, helpers, servant moved there for the duration of the examination.

She qualified – but a girl to the next village? Un thinkable. Un imaginable. So disqualified. Her uncle consoled her."You have studied till matric. How many girls, for that matter how many boys also do we have in our community who have studied that much. What is there in writing an examination. 'Then' I have to find a boy also, who is qualified. And, after studying, are you going to work? Same things you will do as your mother and aunt. Don't feel bad. You will understand later". How, How, How, she pitied herself.

God is kind. Her marriage did not have any element of pity either from her side or others. The best catch those days was, "the boy has a government job, you know". Her uncle made sure of this. A government job in Kanpur. The uncle felt proud, and why not? A three in one combination— good family, good government job and good place (Kanpur --nothing short of going abroad those days).But KARUNA – PITY was yet to be her companion for two more years.

As was the practice those days, the new bride was left behind, to care for the mother-in-law, help the sister–in-laws and bring up the kids in the house hold.

Accepted. The worst part of the pity was, when neighbours with nothing better to do, speculated. Is the stork on its way or not. Now people, specially the women folk did not know physiology or Biology or any logy but they had enough experienceology to understand that couples need to be together for the stork's visit.

On the insistence of her brother-in -law, at last, finally she moved to Kanpur to her husband. Life was wonderful. Everything was different. Everything was new. Everything was good. Some things were 'hers'. Own home, own bedroom, own kitchen, own, own, own, everything down to the floor mat. What a feeling! Never did she feel like this ever in her life. Outings were eye openers. Everything was big, huge, beautiful compared to her little village. Lassi (What was that?), Masala Dosa (Oh! is there something like that), Ice cream (too good. So far ice cream meant those coloured, flavoured, conical ice on a stick) She cherished the moments, savoured every bit of every day.

Life continued. Could she ask for more? That pity syndrome was almost not there. But, There was a but. She lacked cash in her hand. It was a pity. Her husband was loving, caring, respectful and took care of her smallest need, but money he would give only on asking. She had her child and requirement of small change was growing. And all the time, "wait, let your father come in the evening". The little one did not understand. The crunch was felt even more when she visited her village. People looked at her lovely, latest saris, the modern hand bag, the trendy sandals, but when it came to giving something, buying a present, treating her niece and nephews, she was helpless. She was given money but on her return she had to account for it. That was the worst.

It was this, that slowly, that little seed of an idea was trying to burst its way out. She was an excellent cook. She was piled with orders from her friends. "Your payesh (kheer) is delicious. I have a small birthday party for my son, you make the payesh. Or, "Karuna will make the macher jhal (fish cooked in mustard sauce)". There were Bengali bachelors, who were hankering for home food.

All this kept nudging her. She kept debating. Should she? Should she not? Should she? Should she not? Should she share with her husband? What if, he laughs and shoos her away? What if, he thinks, what stupidity. What will the Bengali community comment? What, a dabbawali? Then one day she thought "Enough is enough. To hell with everyone and every one's thought. If her husband agrees good. If he doesn't, forget it".

So the next day,"I want to open a kitchen which will take orders for Bengali food".

He: "But why? We are doing fine, we have enough. We have enough and more".

She: "But look, I slog now and then for other people. It is a talent I have. Why not use it? People need Bengali food here. If I start a Tiffin service here, it will have many takers. It will be an outright success with the bachelors".

He: "Sssh! Can't think of it also. What will people say. Mr. Dutta's wife is into hotel business. No, No forget it".

She: "Let people say anything. You support me. Wait, don't go away. Don't be in a hurry, think it over, please!".

Discussions continued in the morning, while having tea, in the bedroom. So many things to be worked out – Time, place, money, servants, grocery, kitchen equipments --- requirements crowded her mind and brain. 'Where there is a will there is a way' and it happened with her. She started off her entrepreneurial debut with 'Karuna's Kitchen'. Slowly and by God's grace surely, orders came in, bachelors flocked with their food request. 'Karuna's Kitchen' took off. The money started coming in. Yes, she had her own money to keep, save, buy, give, throw away. No more waiting, no more asking. She came out a winner and at last – at last that word pity – karuna was out of her life.

So? What's in a name?.Did some one ask that? Yes, everything is there in a name. Everything is there in us to make that name 'A NAME'.

Blessing in Disguise

Aparupa was crying. Tears rolled down her cheeks nonstop. She was sitting on her bed, leaning against the wall, with a pillow behind her back and she was weeping.

Her second co-sister, Tanushree walked in with a jug of water and stopped abruptly. Surprise written all over her face.

"You are crying still? It is a good forty minutes you have come back from the nursing home. Then on, you are sitting in the same position with tears rolling down your cheeks".

She came and sat near Aparupa, held her chin, "What happened? Tell me. Be out with it. Don't cry like this, how can we help if we do not know what is making you cry and cry so much".

Tanushree got up, called out to her elder co-sister "Didi, Didi", she walked to the door and "Didi come to Rupa's room, do something and stop her crying".

Didi, that is Kajori, arrived wiping her hand in her sari. Held Rupa to her bosom, stroked her hair, kissed her temple and said, "your eyes are swollen with crying. Whatever is troubling or hurting you thrash it out in your mind. If, not sharing helps then don't. But get over it. We don't want you to fall sick. It isn't even an hour you are back from the hospital. Its 9.30, rest now, come down for lunch and three of us will eat together. There is so much of pending gossip. Smile now".

Rupa gave a half smile. More to oblige didi, but there was so much of tears in her heart waiting to burst like a dam and pour down her cheeks.

"Tanu, come with me, let her be for some time. Poor thing! Suffering from the fear that she has a tumor in her stomach, which can be malignant, for the past fifteen, twenty days is taking the toll".

Both left, closing the door silently behind them.

The door closed but the door of her mind opened. And all thoughts, feelings, regrets, misgivings that was bottled inside her for the past fortnight came rushing out. From her leaning, resting position, she let herself slide into a lying position. Tears trickled down from her eyes, over the bridge of her nose, on to the next eyes and down into the pillow.

How could she have such thoughts about Nikhil. Nikhil, her husband for three years. Will God ever forgive her. She cannot forgive herself and she is contemplating God's forgiveness. A fresh bout of tears made her eyes hazy.

Shrabani and she were childhood friends. They lived in the same street, they had the same background, small family, both fathers government servants, both mothers house wives, both went to the same school holding each other's hand, both played seven tiles in the same street, both wore similar colours and clothes. When they grew up they chose the same college and the same subjects. Went for shopping to the same place, read the same books, enjoyed the same movies. Laughed together at the same jokes. They had the same group of friends-both male and female. Among the males was Debashish, who lived just two streets away. Apart from the college group, they made a cozy threesome. They would share notes, debate on 'bamfront' government (left front) go to book exhibitions, exchange novels, celebrate each other's birthdays and best was visiting different pandals during Durgapuja. What fun, those hot hot egg rolls, crispy fish fries, golgappas. Unforgettable days, cherish able moments.

Debashish had a soft corner for her. Never expressed anything explicitly but certain actions showed his liking for her. Like managing to sit next to her during movies, arriving at her door step with hot 'begunis' (brinjal bhajia), on a rainy day. Presenting her with her favourite DVD's. Aparupa enjoyed this subtle attention but never took it seriously. Nor did she encourage Debashish. Actually this, 'as is, where is 'situation was comfortable. She valued his friendship. On the contrary Sharbani, Aparupa felt, no, she knew, had some thing more than friendship towards Debashish. But, Sharbani did not share and Rupa did not ask.

Three of them graduated together and as planned all of them started their post graduation. Two years more of togetherness and sharing. Their focus of discussion now turned to Debashish's job and marriage of both the girls. Everything happened so suddenly. Very first proposal and before anything sank in Aparupa was married to Nikhil Basu, an engineer, own business, flourishing business, own house, car, lived in a joint family with two elder brothers, their wives and children. Aparupa's father, a government servant, belonging to the middleclass, could not ask for more. "It is all your past good deeds" giving all the credit to Aparupa's mother for the successful happening of a great social event called 'daughter's marriage', and 'of course Rupa's good luck 'Bari – Gari- engineer' translated it means house, car and an engineer. Aparupa was consulted. On thinking Aparupa did not find anything to say no.

After her marriage Debashish and Sharbani were together lot more or may be the same amount of time but, being just the two of them, they came closer. Their friendship took a new turn as emotional equations under went a change. He cleared the WBSC exam, became a class II officer in Bengal government with the revenue department. Search for a suitable groom for Sharbani was on, when Sharbani took a bold step forward. On her request Sharbani's father met Debashish's father and by God's grace 'all is well that ends well 'Debashish Sen and Sharbani Mitra were declared man and wife after few months of Aparupa's marriage. Aparupa was of course the closest, most desired, member of the family itself and Nikhil the guest of honour. Anything less is unimaginable. They couldn't believe their luck. How happy they were. The girls laughed less and cried more in their happiness. Aparupa hugged Debashish and said "Thanks for maintaining the trio",

Looking at Nikhil,"Trio plus one" said Debashish. They held each other's hand. "Round of friend ship, no end any where" Sharbani piped in. The rest smiled in agreement.

Did Aparupa know it was the beginning of the heart burn she will suffer every time Sharbani or she talked to Sharbani and days after it also. Right now lying on her bed, recollecting everything, she buried her face into the pillow and burst out once again into uncontrollable tears.

All of them in Kolkata. Such good friends it was a pleasure to think they will meet and chat and share like old times.

First time after Sharbani's marriage they met over a cup of coffee after a little shopping, just like old times. Sharbani could not contain her excitement. She started off exhilaratedly "Rupa, he leaves the minute the office watch

Between You & Me

shows 6 PM. Before marriage I could never imagine making and having tea with someone could be so enjoyable. Rupa, its love …..love and love all the way". "Rupa, he makes great macher kalia, a little overdose of onions but all is fair in love and macher kalia cooked out of love. He insists on cooking the mutton on Sundays, wants me to have an off from the kitchen."

"Rupa I am so happy. So, so happy. Two years back, why two years, even six months back I could have never imagined Debashish would be such a wonderful husband".

They would talk of so many more things but Rupa registered only those that concerned Debashish. Invariably on her way back both Debashish and her husband would be put on the weighing scale and the scale would always tip in Debashish 's favour. Nikhil was not much of a talker. So what? Shouldn' t he share more about his business, his day to day life in the office, what happened, where he went, what he did, just like Debashish. She recalled Nikhil saying, "Every day in the office is routine Rupa, but yes, the day something different happens I wait to come home and tell you".

But Aparupa argued with her inner voice, 'Why should he wait for that special day. He should talk every day like ……Forget it'. And coming home? The three brothers arrived for dinner earliest by eight. The wives would finish watching their different TV serials, sometimes get busy in their rooms, Children's home work, knitting, reading and then the bell would announce the brothers arrival. Aparupa thought,' Why wait for the brothers, Nikhil can come home early, like Debashish at 6 O'clock, Lucky Sharbani. They must be going out also. The last time she rang, she told how they had gone for this theatre show. She is up to date with the latest movies too. And here was she, movies, theatres, exhibitions would come and go and where was Nikhil –at office. And the three co– sisters managed a movie or shopping or visiting a relative on their own. She told herself Nikhil was Nikhil. His job different, his family different, his requirements different. But that would be for a moment. Her mind would again go back to comparing the husbands –hers and Sharbanis. And every time she saw Nikhil in a shade darker than Debashis. "Hello! Rupa come to our favourite joint. We have just returned from Puri, I have so much to tell you". Aparupa got ready lethargically to meet Sharbani. When was the last time they, Nikhil and Rupa, went for a holiday? The whole family, brothers, wives children, all had gone to Goa. Why does she get into this comparison mode? What does she want to prove to herself? Nikhil is not as good as Debashish. Or Nikhil is better than Debashish. And how does it matter? Nikhil is Nikhil and Debashish is debashish.

The minute the two friends met Sharbani was gushing.

"Rupa, the sea, Debashish and I, there cannot be a better combination. Rocking Rupa rocking ….." Sharbani went on and on and on. Rupa's eyes were on sharbani and her mind was in Goa. The holiday. Sharbani was saying some thing about being dragged into the water, a similar scene emerged -----

"Come, the sea is great" Nikhil.

"No chance. This is a new Salwar Kameez I have worn" Rupa.

"Come feel the sea. There is no sea in Kolkata". Nikhil.
"No, No".

"Not coming? Sure?" Nikhil had something in his eyes. Thrill? Adventure? Teasing? Before Rupa could say NO a second time he just lifted her and walked into the sea.

Next moment both were dripping salt water all over, her co – sisters, brother in laws, kids, who were already knee deep in the water, started clapping enjoying their youngest uncle and aunts gimmicks. Passersby stopped to enjoy the family film.

"It's great shopping with Deb, Rupa, he wants me to buy every thing. I bought a sari for you too".

She pushed a packet in front of Rupa. "Red and black Kotki, you will look gorgeous".

………'You look gorgeous, never seen you like this before, can't take my eyes of you' the word gorgeous and Rupa was back to memory lane. Nikhil said this when she wore the long skirt and those typical T shirts you get in Goa with the sun and the palm print. This was a different Nikhil, not the 9 to 9 Kolkata office Nikhil. She should treasure and be happy with such recollections and not reminisce only when confronted by Sharbani with Debashish details. Rupa felt guilty and reprimanded herself for not remembering all those other holidays to Peling and Kalimpong, Delhi, Kanyakumari and so many others. How can she forget her out of the world honey moon to Mandu. And why did Nikhil choose Mandu? Of course for the unforgettable love story of Rani Roopmati and Muslim King Baz Bahadur. How can she push aside these lovely moments of her love and married life and like an obsessed fool only dwell on Sharbani and Debashish. She felt miserable. Thank God nobody can make out what is in others mind. How would Nikhil feel if he could read her mind and know what she was juggling in her mind all the time.

……… "Yes, and two plates of prawn curry also". Nikhil ordered.

"Of course, of course, how can Nikhil forget prawns. Some ones favourite dish" the elder co- sister piped in.

Nikhil quiet, subtle, had his own ways of manifesting his love and affection for Rupa. Rupa knew it too, but ----- there should not be any but, Debashish was not the measuring rod for Nikhil.

Durga Puja. That festival in which all Bengalies 9 to 90, plunged in as if that year is going to be the last Durga Puja or it is their first Durga Puja. Month and more, before and after it, all conversations, happenings, activities, cleaning, shopping, visiting, and what not is around Durga Puja. Durga Puja, the yearly life line of all Bengalies. They live from one Durga Puja to the next. And why not? It rejuvenates. It relaxes. It connects. It brings life to a full circle. Happy and complete.

Sharbani and Aparupa rang each other at regular intervals or they met. Saris to wear, saris to be given, Sari for Shashti (sixth day of the festival), Sari to be worn on Ashtomi (eigthth day of the festival), their accessories. Mini and mega plans for the puja days. Hyper activities ensued both in Basu and Mitra households. In fact Rupa felt one up (but why?) as in their house hold along with all the shopping came a piece of jewellery too. A 'choker' or a 'churi' or a 'bala' was a regular affair. They indulged in their women folk. It was not a show of affluence, this gift of gold, a bonus, which came with love and affection attached to it.

There ended Aparupa's ecstasy. Next sentence from Sharbani burst her balloon of feeling good.

"What plans for the nights?"

A regular practice with Kolkata Bengalis is to visit puja pandals in the cool of the nights. Crowd 'long queues', being awake till the wee hours of the morning did not deter them.

They were on the streets ---park street to Talapark in hordes "What plans for the nights? "Sharbani continued, "The first day, that is shashti Debashish and I will come home. Ma wants us. Meet you then, we will plan something together".

"Then?" Rupa asked. "Saptomi we will enjoy by ourselves" and she winked. Rupa kept looking.

"Next two days we will go to Ma –in –law. Rupa her food is simply awesome. I am just waiting to gorge on it, get decked in the evenings and enjoy the night out with the family and of course Mr Debashish Mitra. Too too good". Aparupa nodded in agreement. "Your Plan?"

"No outings Sharbani. It is the custom in our house, Daughters come to stay with their mother, just like Maa Durga visiting her Maykaa. It is a lot of fun, you can feel the festival. The house is filled with mirth, children's laughter and the aroma of luchi, aloor dom and payesh. We become even more busy with the kitchen. You can imagine, two sister –in –laws, their husbands, children and add all of us also".

"Wow!" Sharbani exclaimed and added "and a pile of gifts too".

"Yes, yes", Rupa replied.

Returning home Aparupa thought why can't Nikhil simply tell every body 'I and Rupa are going out'. He will never do it. Sisters are his life and the sisters –they dote on Nikhil. The first year of marriage itself he had declared "our puja is more of a home affair with all the brothers, sisters, boudis and the jamai babus and the little ones". He added."You will like it Rupa. You will feel the family bond".

And Rupa liked it too. Till Sharbani came along with all the stories.

She remembered how Nikhil would stand holding her plate while she ate the 'Phuchkas'. How, while all walked ahead he would hold her hand and smile down on her. Shield her with his arm when the crowd was too much. Hold her hand bag while she knotted her hair into a bun. Such tender moments, they were there, strewn all around her. She had to just close her eyes to feel those warm loving moments. But she would only cud –chew on what Sharbani said, what Sharbani did, what Sharbani shared.

This went on and on. It was becoming an obsession with her. No day passed without such rumination.

Then this happened. She had to be rushed to the nursing home. Heavy bleeding and unbearable pain. It was like this for the past six months or so. But like all women, what was important, a check up, was ignored. Let 's see, next month and next month. When Aparupa shared with Nikhil at night, he sat up, his face so worried that had it not been night 11 he would have dragged Rupa to their family physician then and there. But Rupa could not forget and will never forget all her living years. Nikhil's face. So tense as if Rupa was struck by a terminal disease. As if the Judge just delivered a death sentence.

She laughed. "Sleep now Nikhil It happens some time or the other with all ladies". But the whole night she could not sleep because he was so restless by her side. She never saw him anything like this anytime before.

"Nikhil, not sleepy?"

"Tomorrow the first thing we will do is go to the doctor. Don't get into the kitchen. Don't get involved in any house work".

"Oh!" Rupa said "you are still thinking about it?"

"Don't fall sick Rupa. Don't be sick. I want to come back home every day and see you smiling back from the kitchen, or the bedroom or laying the table for dinner".

"Look at the way you are talking. I am not sick. I am fine, just a little problem. Stop worrying so much". She held him close as if holding him will transfer his anxiety to her. "Sleep now".

From the next day started the harassing time like nothing on earth. Doctors, specialists, sonography, X-rays, imaging, scanning for that little growth she had in her uterus. Morning it was one hospital, evening it was another. Series of tests. Everybody spent sleepless nights. Would it be benign or malignant? What if malignant? The thought of it sent the whole household into depression. Everybody talked less, laughed less or was it Rupa's imagination. She took it in her stride and always waited for all her test results with resilence. But the worst hit was Nikhil.

Her husband was like a person possessed. No office, no work. His days revolved around Rupa. His only concern was Rupa. What to do for her, how can she be more comfortable, how quickly she can be cured, can another opinion help, is there an alternative medicine rather than surgical intervention. He was by her side day in and day out. Nobody could convince him to have some rest or have some sleep.

Rupa was seeing a new Nikhil. No, not a new Nikhil. Nikhil was the same. Everything, his love, his emotions, his possessiveness, his care was hidden. With this crisis it came out in the open. But all the time it was there. Only Rupa did not see the Nikhil that she should have seen. She searched in her husband all those unimportant, irrelevant qualities and in the bargain what happened? She alone suffered those unwanted qualms.

What a mistake!. Where was she wandering in her stupid world of superficiality. How foolish she was not to see the gem that was Nikhil. So many wasted years in comparison. So many months gone, so many days missed, so many moments lost, all because of her.

Finally it was decided, benign or malignant, the tumor need to be removed. When she went into the OT she could not forget his face. It was lifeless. She wanted to run to him, into his arms and say "forgive me, forgive me, I want to be back here". She was wheeled in, her eyes still on her husband's face and his eyes trying to hold on to hers till the door closed. When she came out, Nikhil's concerned, worried face was waiting.

Reports of the tumor was negative. What a relief it was for the whole family. Rupa realized how lucky she was to belong to such a family, where co-sisters were more mothers than co- sisters and brother -in - laws were brothers and no in- laws was attached. Days of taking care followed. Nikhil left it to no one. Rupa's eyes followed him everywhere. The more she saw him, the more she loved him and more she hated herself.

Holding the spoon of medicine "This is what is great about all living together. A joint family and a joint business. How long have I not gone to the office Rupa?"

When the food came for both of them from home she thanked God for giving such angels as her co- sisters.

"There is something very …… very sexy" Nikhil looked at Rupa, "dressing your wife, though sick".

"Nikhil shut up. what a mind you have".

"Rupa, thank God I have a mind. When I came to know about your tumor and the following surgery I thought I would become mindless".

Be it medicines, changing, sponging, adjusting the pillow, helping her to stretch, taking her to the washroom, Nikhil was there.

Her co – sister Kajori said, "Rupa, is he combing your hair also?"

Rupa laughed. "That's remaining", Laughing again "I will …."

Nikhil interrupted, "fine, where is the comb? Good you reminded me Boudi".

Days of light bantering and getting well continued. Rupa was in love with her husband all over again. But when she thought about herself she had this strong urge to burst into tears. In the nursing home she often controlled herself.

Today morning she was discharged. She came home with Nikhil. He settled her.

"Should I go to the office today?" He looked at her intently trying to gauge her need and comfort level. "or…. Should I hang around my lovely wife for two days more? I, actually don't mind. Order and I am available". He bowed mockingly. That is when tears rolled down her cheeks uncontrollably.

"Here, here, what happened now? You are fine, you are home Rupa".

"Nothing. Just being back home, back to my room, being with you. I cant express Nikhil. I feel like laughing and crying at the same time. Hold me Nikhil. Hold me tight". Nikhil held her tenderly. Ran his fingers through her hair.

"I always thought my dear wife was a little mad but now I know, how wrong I was".

Rupa looked at him enquiringly. "Now I know there is nothing little, she is fully mad".

"Thank your stars I am confined to bed, other wise you could not have got away with such a comment".

"so ma'am, office or no office?"

"Go. Brothers need you in office. A change of scene will be good for you".

"My best scene is in front of me. What better scene do I need?"

Tears welled up once again. "oh wait, wait. At this rate the Kolkata police will use me instead of tear gas shells". He left for office. In the quietness of her room she cried on. Intervention by her co- sisters did not help. Tears flowed unbarringly.

That night, in their room, "Why Rupa", he held her close "bad days are over, we are together, what more?"

"yes what more". She hugged him, buried her face in his chest, smelt the familiar talcum he used, in her mind she said,

"Nikhil Forgive me for not knowing you".

"Nikhil Forgive me for being blind". "Nikhil Forgive me for not understanding".

"Nikhil Forgive me for being such an infidel, even if it is in the mind".

"Nikhil Forgive me for thinking if you were my right choice".

He tried to disentangle from her embrace, but in her sleep also she held on, not letting him go. When he saw her smooth, unlined face, he let her be.

After a week or so "Hello!"

"Rupa here. Sharbani you?"

"How are you? Oh! We were all so worried. Traumatic, No? Rupa you are laughing!!!"

"Yes I am. It was a blessing in disguise".

A shocked Sharbani over the phone, "Blessing?"

"Yes. You won' t understand", she kept the phone, leaned against the wall, with a smile on her lips and let out a deep sigh.

The Award

Most of us try our hand at writing, be it prose, poetry an essay or may be a travelouge. Especially in our younger days. Later of course wisdom dawns and we come to know how unsuitable we are for such a spree. How inadequate is our vocabulary. How inappropriate is our use of language.

Why should I be an exception? So the minute I could match 'fate—date' 'kneel –feel', 'glow –flow', I was writing poetry left, right and centre. The best part of it was, there were takers. My school magazine, the Durga Puja souvenir –among many advertisements of ornaments, paints, steel tubes and chemicals, my poem 'Goddess Durga' would be there, my father's office in-house magazine. Because the magazine had a family section I made my entry there.

I grew. Good or bad, my urge to write also grew. Whenever I felt something, whatever came to my mind, I penned it down. Some I kept. Some I threw away as trash.

Then came the college magazine. Here the exposure was better, so was the criticism. I was mature enough then to take the accolades with the brick bats. In the mean time I also realized, I liked writing. Very philosophically, I also realized 'work (that is write) –don't wait for the reward'. I was also an avid reader. News papers, magazines, paper backs, fictions, thrillers, religious discourses from Ramayan- Mahabharat to Osho, from Leon Uris to Jhumpa Lahiri, Arvind Adiga,

Chetan Bhagat, Khaled Hosseini et al. Bengali magazines, 'Pujo barshikis' (yearly magazines published during Durga Puja with all the writings of the best Bengali writers) Bengali authors, old and new. I read them. I became awed. How beautifully they wrote. How smoothly the language flowed. How expressively they conveyed emotions, feelings, incidents. They played with humour and seriousness with equal ease. Serenity, peace, love, hatred, you could feel them all. Then it dawned on me –writing for your own pleasure and writing for yourself and others to enjoy are two things going at a tangent. And for an author to combine them together and making a meaningful piece of reading material is no joke. My inner voice told me, so far so good, don't you dream any more, come down to earth, work, look after your husband, family, cook, keep house and be happy. Thank the Durga Puja souvenir, school and college magazine for giving you that little space where your literary work (can I call it that) was show cased. I agreed with my inner voice but that urge to write could not be suppressed by my head. My head over ruled, so, I thought, 'what harm, if I keep penning down my thoughts, feelings, observations, realizations that I want to see in black and white. Experiences that I would like to remember'. So I continued writing, whenever I had the time, things happened or just because I felt like.

Children, apple of our eyes, can be such horrors. The brother and sister would smirk and say, "bhaiyya, you see the cup of coffee? You see the full scape note book and the pen? Mamma is in the process of creating another literary master piece".

The brother's retort is worse. "Ssssssssh. It is the best thing to happen for us, at least we will be spared from her Hitchkockian scrutiny". Some times I would find a placard on my table "Savdhaan!! Work in progress. Sorry! Sorry! Literary Work in progress". Who else can come up with such remarks other than my own, precious off springs. At such times my husband looked at me indulgently. His pleading eyes told the children, 'let her be. Don't be after her'.

But nothing deterred me. I ploughed through – often dreaming about my progress and the final culmination into an author. At least I had the right to dream.

In the mean time, some women's magazines featured my articles. If three were accepted, for six there were no acknowledgement. Accepted or discarded not known. I wish magazines do inform the budding writers where they stand. I hope they understood how crucial their 'yes' or 'no' was and mattered to these aspiring writers. But I guess they are too involved reading, contemplating other works of more promising or well known people. Now and then, a small writing of mine would be in print with my name. And those were the days, my friends, I thought would never end. Open the book at least twenty times a day, read it again and again as if, if I did not read it, the article would vanish. It would accompany me everywhere. To the drawing room, to the kitchen, to the swing outside. Once again pages would be turned to make myself believe this is what I wrote and there is my name. The last journey would be to the bedroom. Under the bed room light, I would read it for the last time for the day, keep it on the bedside table, give out a sigh and go to sleep. I am sure there would be a small smile on my lips too. But I cannot see my own smile, can I? The next day I would start my day not with 'Vishnu Sahasranamam' but with the magazine on page 63. One small thing would be there written by Shilpi Dutta. What pleasure, what satisfaction, it gave to watch my own name.

Yes, the day would be made and I would begin, I would start with new vigour. Too many ideas would be running crazy in my head and they would once again take shape in the form of words and sentences.

My children too became tolerant. The brother says "No jokes. Mamma's articles are published, okay".

"They are not bad too. We like them". Comes from the sister sheepishly.

What should I say? Thank God for small mercies. My husband continued with that indulgent look. 'I am there beside you'. His silent look assured me. Life continued, writing continued. Happiness when my articles got a place in some magazine. Rejection brought dejection. But by now I had become a die hard, no one could stop me from writing.

Days passed giving way to months and months to years. I was deep into my morning puja. I was getting ready to place my long list of demand to God, when the door bell rang. It rang again and again. 'Some impatient fellow at the door. No peace' I thought to myself. I came down and opened the door and invariably there stood before me the courier chap. He was smiling. Otherwise you have those grumpy fellows, whose facial expression tells you how late you are in opening the door and in the process wasting his precious time. Signed duly and taken I, as usual, placed it on the dining table. Thinking,'Oh! One of those numerous investment statements that tells my husband, he is as rich or as poor as before'. But the envelope looked different. It was not announcing any flat 50% discount. It had a very official look about it. It was addressed to me. Curiosity took over. I picked the envelope back and turned it around in my hand. There was a shiver in my hands, my eyes were big rounds of surprise and I was becoming a little breathless.

It was a white envelope, with my name and address formally printed and the envelope announced it was from the 'Society of Amateur Writers'. Yes, the letter was meant for me. I opened it with trembling hands. The letters were blurred. I read it once, twice, thrice. Was I reading right? I had a good grasp of the English language. I could not be understanding wrong. Immediately, as I could not bear it any more, I rang my panacea for all problems – my husband.

"Asim, listen. The Society for Amateur Writers have liked my articles and they have decided to recognize my efforts by giving me a cash award of Rs 10,000 and a citation. They will also take me for a workshop in Delhi for a fortnight. Wait, I have not finished. The award will be given to fifty others like me. The function will be in Delhi. I cannot believe, I will receive the prize from Ashutosh Lahiri. Contemporary author, his books have been filmed also. Recognized and praised abroad too".

When my children heard, their faces were flushed. They hugged me tight. Showered me with the best of adjectives.

Then began the hectic days of planning. Booking tickets, accommodation, what to wear. What to wear, nothing can be more important than this gigantic decision. Painful and enjoyable at the same time.

"This cream sari?"

"Very simple and a little dull too"

"The maroon Kanjivaram?"

"Too grand. It is not a wedding. Wear a nice dhakai sari like a true Bengali" opined my husband. Phone calls, friends, relatives, all called, congratulated and the best part of it is, they said, they all knew 'I had it in me'.

I wanted my husband to accompany me. He too was invited.

At last the D –Day. In the morning I felt feverish. My legs and hands were not moving in tandem with my brain and vice–versa. After every two minutes I looked at Asim. In this state I got ready. We took a cab to the venue. It was a small, formally decorated, somber looking hall. Few had already arrived. I walked nervously with Asim to the place meant for me. I thanked God for creating a species called husband, who was now beside me giving me that unseen support. Others arrived. Not a small crowd either. I looked around. Did everyone feel as I felt? Why do people talk in whispers? It makes you even more jittery.

The function began with a small prayer. The guest of honour spoke. I listened attentively. The school girl in me was back, soaking in every word the speaker spoke. These tips, hints would be my future guide.

Then the award giving ceremony began. My name was called. I got up, moved as gracefully as possible with a smile on my lips. I extended my hand to receive the award.

"Mamma, Mamma, Mamma, wake up. Wake up Ma. What are you smiling in your sleep and extending your hand for".

I got up from my doze. Back to my first floor, TV room rocking chair. How could I tell my daughter I was dreaming, and in my dream I was extending my hand to accept an award.

Instead I told her, "Sweetu I had a lovely dream. AND I am going to make that dream come true. I WILL".

MNC

These days we have umpteen books telling you five effective ways to make your bitter, Sorry! better half happy, ten good reasons why you should be a vegetarian or hundred ways to help your child succeed. If not a book at least an article to tell you a few good reasons why you should marry a man from a MNC.

Multi National Company. If we do not know about them we are neither liberalized nor globalized. That is what was said in the 1990's. And it is true. Read and find out how. Of course from a house wives point of view. That is important. Have you not seen in the latest election agendas on the TV, 50 % of us are women.

First and foremost, most MNC executive bachelors have all those excellent academic records, which you have always dreamt of in the man you were going to marry. Distinctions galore, few gold medals, first in this and topped in that. So, once you are married to an MNC man you can very correctly be all your friend's, neighbour's and relative's (Specially those with marriageable daughters) envy. May be this was what you dreamt of even more. (sorry, ye bhi koi share karne ki baat hai?)

Secondly, all those women who start crying even before they have chopped onions and have a headache at the thought of making tea, the MNC executive is the right choice. He will remain out 20 days in a month, so, you can settle down to watching the best soap on TV with that quick sandwich or two minute noodles or Pav –bhaji from the nearest fast- food joint. Is'nt it great, you are married, you are Mrs so and so and no cooking, cutting, frying and sautéing.

Again, married to a MNCian, you get to be known to be the best of house keepers. People admire your tastefully kept drawing room, efficient kitchen, homely living space, comfortable guest room and what not. Since your MNC husband is most of the time out, you have ample time to shine your brass, vacuum your carpet, and press your curtains. In fact a list can be made like this, Monday he is in Madras, clean steel cupboard, Tuesday he is in Tuticorin, clean crockery, Wednesday he is in Warrangal, change linen. So on and so forth. Isn't it comfortable?

Being a multinational company your husband will definitely go abroad for some meeting, some training or just spending the companies money (don't take it seriously). This is the time, you can ring up your not- so- friendly friend to tell her how lonely you are with your husband so f----a----r away in Sweden or Switzerland. You can tell your inquisitive and prying neighbor, how he is going to be away in Germany for two months. With these visits Toblerone will become a household name and your drawing room will proudly display crystals from Sweden, Murano glass from Italy. Your friends will announce their visit by ringing the Swiss bell hanging out on your door. Children will be happy to have papa away for all those lovely remote control cars and toys plus the Legoland kits thrown in.

MNC's do things in style. They take their executives to extravagant holiday destinations (sometimes wives included)

Between You & Me

for workshops. Work cum pleasure or work with pleasure, whatever the motive. The yearly parties and get togethersare all out of the world in out of the world places. The executive and his family get the best of perks in the form of air travel, soft furnishings, hard furnishings, soft loans for car, house, a soft cushy life that is. On transfers, the HR department will make sure that ordinary children get their admission in extra ordinary schools. While you flick through your favourite fashion magazine (contemplating your next buy) the packers and movers would have done it all..You can choose the best of houses in the best of localities. Rent? Not to bother, your MNC will take care of it.

The list is endless. But listen to this and don't say I did'nt warn you. It happened to me and it could happen to you also. My dear hubby was away for a long stint. I and my little one was having dinner when there was a knock on the door. "go see who is there".Sonny came back and said "One uncle is calling you".Iwent out and to my surprise what do I see? The father is at the door. Father has become an uncle, a stranger. See what long absence does to the children.. Aisa bhi hota hai.

Hajam nahi hua? Then have a Hajmola sir.

You cannot forget Preeti

There are verses which remain incomplete. There are words which convey no meaning. There are roads which come to a dead end. There are thoughts which remain unspoken. So………..should I or should I not write about her. It is not going to tickle anyone (as humorous articles do). It is not going to make someone think (as thought provoking articles do).It is not going to activate your grey cells (as puzzles & riddles do). But, yes it will make you think, you will question "Why God, it has to be like this, sometimes?"

That was my first year of teaching. I walked into the bustling noisy class of XI commerce. Immediate silence. Each sizing me up in their own way—I in turn sizing each of them in my own way and then ---there she was. What struck me most was her sparkling, smiling eyes. She was short, not very fair, a round face (which as I came to know more- became a round, intelligent face) nice, jet black hair, neatly plaited, looking smart in the school uniform, giving a small welcoming smile to me. The first thought that crossed my mind was 'That should be a nice girl'.

As days passed to make weeks & weeks to become months, I was well into teaching & the schools way of life. I discovered I liked her more & more every passing day. Never would she forget to wish, never was there a day she was not smiling. Respectful & obedient, I came to know, she was not only my favourite but liked by many other teachers.

She came, she saw & she conquered her fellow students. She had joined just that year and got elected as the vice head girl. Very good for a new comer. When it came to sitting, she sat last, when it came to marks, she came first. I can still picture that face in the last bench ---satisfied, when she understood, screwed up, when she did not, knitted brows, when she was confused. She expressed her view point with full gusto. She loved her Economics classes for all the discussions that could take place. "Why ma'am do we not have only labour intensive techniques?". "Why ma'am we should go off to other countries, when there is so much work to be done here?". "Why ma'am they do not teach law at school"? On lighter discussions, "Why ma'am women should do all the house work?" or "Why can't men stay with their wife's parents after marriage?". And many, many more whys and all the whys, that interesting.

Very motivated, very enthusiastic and very ambitious. First the twelfth, then bachelors, next the masters then the competitive exams to become an IAS officer. All plans chalked out and ready. She was naughty too. First to ask for a free period, first to close her note book and start chatting. A good debator, she would practice umpteen times till perfect. On my birthday, on our new year, she would be there "Ma'am shubho nabo borsho", wishing me in typical Bengali style.

After the annual exams, she came gushing to me, "Ma'am guess what? This holiday, I have decided to visit all my grandparents, uncles, aunts, cousins, everybody. So nice na ma'am!!"

Like all vacations, summer vacations ended even before it began. My second year in school, I was more than eager to join back, meet friends, exchange news. And then someone said "You know Sikha …..". Oh God! how can that be?!!! One so young, one so full of life, of all things chicken pox and a few days fever. When I entered the class, that face was not there. That face did not smile back at me. That face was not there to wish me. That face which questioned me, which made me so happy, would not be there any more. It was hard for me, it was not the same class any more. Teaching the class was not fun anymore.

Then I questioned "Why God, why does it have to be like this sometimes?".

Final Decision

Sitting at the table waiting for his next patient, DrBidhanChaudhury thought of the jelly fish story for the third time. Third time in three hours, in spite of 4 to 5 patients. The last sentence, 'it made a difference to this one and this one and this one …………' came back to him every time a patient left the room. Actually it did not come back, it was there at the back of his mind, correction, on his mind all the time. His wife Ananya knew about the turmoil he was going through. As always, always supportive, always there when he needed her, always not there when he wanted it that way. She, as usual, with that understanding smile, held his hand and told "Don't hurry, you will get your answer and that answer will be the right one". How he loved her. How much he loved her. Today he loved her even more, because he knew, whatever his answer, she will be there beside him. He needed her assuring presence and her understanding smile even more –today

Dr.Bidhan Chaudhury, in his IXth standard, his father, a quiet man, with a personality which automatically commanded sense of awe and respect, called him to his study.

"I have named you Bidhan, so that one day you can be a Doctor like him, DrBidhan Chandra Roy and be known for your service to the people. We cannot aspire to be like him but he can be the light you can follow. If you happen to achieve even a small percentage of his ideals, that day will be a proud day for me. Have this" he extended a book of DrBidhan Chandra Roy's life and achievements to him.

Today, after three decades his father's words came back to him. He could see that half dark, half lighted room, his father's reclining figure in the easy chair and his words rang clearly in his ears as if hewas being spoken to now. Serve, serve the people. That was what he desired. That was what he wanted. The story came back to him once again. A man walked in the beach where hundreds of jelly fish were thrown ashore. Most died, unable to swim back. This man, as he walked, picked some of them and threw them back into the sea. A boy noticed this for days. One day he walked upto him and said,

"Hundreds of them die, what are you doing, throwing a few of them into the sea? What difference does it make?"

The man picked a jelly fish and threw it into the sea, the fish swam to life. He said, "It made a difference to this one". Picked up the next, it went into the sea, "It made a difference to this one also". The boy said, "Understood".

His father's words and 'the man and the jelly fish', he knew his decision will make a difference. He stood up, forgetting his waiting patients, suddenly he felt light, as if a big weight had been lifted off his shoulder. He had made up his mind, he clearly saw his future life, what awaited him, and what he wanted to take up eagerly, so eagerly that he never remembered himself looking forward to something this eagerly. When did it all begin? This restlessness, This debate?. Some two years back. May be little more. It began with his small holiday in 'Shibnibas'. A small village in interior West Bengal, 14 kms away from Bangladesh border. Shib-Nibas --Abode of Lord Shiva. Named because of a Shiv temple built by Raja Krishnachandra. But how did he land there? Wanting to spend some tranquil time in that village with pristine beauty given by its green paddy fields, greener mango orchards, winding muddy roads and the flowing river "Churni". He visited, re-visited and all his visits slowly and surely confirmed the conviction in his heart of hearts, which was growing larger by every passing day.

In that village lived and practiced his Doctor friend Dr.Kunal Dutta.

An usual day. Actually a good day. He felt his wallet in his back pocket. Heavy and fat with notes. He had a good practice as a thoracic surgeon. By God's grace he had a good name in the market, adoctor with the healing touch. Patients came, their friends and relatives came, old patients sent in new patients. He had nothing to complain. He was driving his new car, a Honda Accord, and going home for lunch. Thought of home brought a smile to his face. Thought of Ananya, waiting for him always spread a warmth through his whole being, at those moments he could think of nothing but only raise his eyes heaven wards and thank God for giving him Ananya. How well the name suited her. Ananya –uncomparable. To him she was Ananya.

He stopped at the traffic light, tapping his fingers on the steering, looked around. Not so crowded at this time of the day, but the sari shops always do brisk business whatever the time of the day. Ladies!!! He smiled to himself. Smiling at his train of thought he leisurely turned left. Is that Kunal? Kunal Dutta, his MBBS batch mate, later while Kunalstudied further for Medicine, he himself branched off to Surgery.

"Hey Kunal" he shouted across the window.

"Bidhan!!, Hello! look the lights have turned green".

"Koi baat nahi". (That is no problem) "Drive and stop at left. I'll follow".

They met. Exchanged -- How, Where, why, when of things. Kunal had come to Kolkata to replenish his stock of medicine. Both felt the need to be together, to talk, to remember. Bidhan got Kunal to come home the same night for dinner (the next morning Kunal was leaving).

Bidhan had a house in Lake town. A neat little house, cosy and comfortable with a little patch of green in front, an unthinkable luxury in a metropolis. Full credit to Ananya for making the inside equally beautiful. Tastefully decorated. Every bit, the furniture, the carpet and the curtains, the artifacts, all carefully chosen. Bidhan's house showed Ananya's love and care for it. Every corner had a feeling of home.

Kunal, in the evening, when he came for dinner, appreciated and complimented both Bidhan and Ananya. Dinner over. Three of them sat with coffee. Bengali dinner replete with veg, non- veg, sweet and that inevitable 'mishti doi' (sweet yogurt) leaves no place for coffee, but so much more to exchange after a gap of so many years, 'coffee toh banta hai'.

Bidhan talked about his private clinic, his twenty bed nursing home, the latest two medical equipment, that he added. His son, who was in the third year of medicine. Kunal talked about his choice of the village for further medical practice, his exposure to village medical demands, his experience there. His wife Tripti was a physiotherapist. During their courtship they had agreed, the village would be there 'Karmabhoomi'. They, like Bidhan and Ananya, too feel they were made for each other. Blessed with two daughters, one was into medicine and the other into literature—growing up in the village and fed by Tagore and Sarat Chandra, she had only one direction, that is Bengali Literature.

They did not realize a good four hours had passed. They parted-- on a very hopeful note. Bidhan and Ananya would visit Kunal and his wife after Durga Puja. Usually Bidhan took a few daysoff then, exclusively to be with family. So, those days were calendar marked for Kunal – Tripti – Shibnibas. Bidhan had no inkling then, when he promised to visit Shibnibas, that it would be a turning point in his life. Rather it would be a point which would turn his life.

After this, both friends were regularly in touch. sometimes exchanging pleasantries, enquiring after each other and family. At times they talked shop –ailments, treatments, special medical cases, medicines. Bidhan kept his promise and right after "Bijoya Dashami" his car headed for Shibnibas early in the morning. They reached Shibnibas at about 11 or 11. 20. There was a stillness in the air apart from the cooing of a distant koel or the cawing of a crow. The river flowed silently, its greenish water shimmering at places from the sunlight. "Looks like as if a green sequined sari is spread out" Said Ananya. Bidhan chided in reply "Oh ho! already poetic". A gentle breeze blew, rustling the branches and leaves. A stray dog headed busily in some direction in search of food. A vigilant, protective mother hen with her chicks was around the hedge of Kunal'shouse. A man in a muddy dhoti on a depreciated cycle passed, then stopped, typically villagish, then shot out a number of enquiries –who Bidhan was, where was he going, are they from the 'Shahor' (city) etc, etc till his curiosity was satisfied. Bidhan was amused, enjoyed answering the inquisitive passerby. Kunal, Tripti with their daughters were waiting. After a big round of Hi's, Hello's and hugs they all settled for that every Bengalis luxury - - Darjeeling tea.

The greenness of the surroundings overwhelmed them. They loved it. It was seeping in to their skin and soul. They were glad they made it to this place, such a place still existed was beyond their imagination. They had become so much of city people. The place soothed them from minute one. Bidhan got up and stretched, all of them walked to the garden. Fruits and flowers galore. Their shade and fragrance making the place heavenly. Kunal had a house more in tune with village requirement. In front, was a long hall, one end had Kunal's clinic, table, chair and all the knick knacks of a medical practitioner, the middle portion had two examining beds plus those things that were needed for first aid, preliminary treatment. The other end had four hospital beds for admitting patients over night or for a few days.

"I don't need anything more", "This room takes care of all the medical needs of the villages".

"Villages?"

"Yes, there is only one health center here, with one fresh doctor, forced to serve the village before earning his degree and one qualified nurse. They are over worked and the facilities a little too inadequate. So I am welcome by many of the villages around. There is a continuous flow of patients day and night".

"Why night?"

"Yes, I am open twenty four hours. There are cases of snake bites, old people falling (being unable to see well at night), suddenly sick children, women and so many more. Don't be shocked. Twenty four hours open sounds shocking but it is always not twenty four hours. And I have got used to it also. I have chosen the village as my work place. Bidhan I want to be available, I want to be there when I am needed". For the first time for a fleeting moment Bidhan thought, can he speak like this, like Kunal. He brushed aside such thoughts. He has come here to refresh, re-energise, relax and not to get into such disturbing questions. He looked at

Ananya. Ananya too looked so care free. There was not a line of worry on her face.

The inner house was simple but even more beautiful. Its design, arrangement was such that it had all the city amenities, but well adapted to the village as well. The house gave a feeling of belonging, a feeling of being together. May be Bidhan's vision was coloured. At the first sight he liked everything about the place, may be that liking was extended to the house as well. No harm. It is good to feel good. Right in the centre was a twenty by twenty space. That was the dining place. Unique, it had a glass roof covered from the outside by a growing, flowering creeper. There was sun and there was shade. Night or day, you felt your meals were under a tree. All the time the place was chirpy, people flitting in and out, having tea, food, reading the paper, conversing with others. Around it on three sides were four rooms, on one side the kitchen. The best part of the kitchen was, it had three and a half refrigerators. Three big ones, one small. Ananya looked at Tripti questioningly.

"One fridge for the family and two and a half for his medicines". Kunal was leaning against the kitchen door, spoke.

"Remember, when we met I told you, I visited Kolkata every month for medicines. I get them and stock it up in these fridges. Most of the time one trip is sufficient. The place, it seems was slowly seeping into city practitioner Dr. Bidhan. Or is it being away from the usual surrounding of home, crowded streets, busy days, clinic, this was a welcome change. Again he brushed aside such thoughts and said to himself 'enjoy, make the most of the few days'. The three days that he stayed, he also helped Kunal with the various patients – stomach problems, injuries, heat boils, aches and pains of various kinds and parts. Most common was fever due to cold. Too much of the river I guess, Bidhan thought to himself. It also came to his mind --- Not much challenge. Not much challenge? Really? He did not know how challenge emerged in the village. He was most touched by the devotion of the villagers. Kunal's word was final. His touch was enough. They looked upon him as god sent. No questions, no arguments, blind belief and faith. If you have reached "DaktarBabu" all health problems will be settled and cured. He was not complaining. His patients were his bread and butter. But, city patients, so many questions. Literate lot, they have a good amount of knowledge about illness and medicines, convincing was a job more than the treatment itself. Anyway, pros and cons are always there, he is not going to have a mental debate on practice in the village versus practice in the city. There was a slight chill in the air, the breeze from the river side a degree colder, but refreshing. they were all enjoying their morning chat over tea and biscuits. "I will really miss this solitude. I am going to be your regular guest, so get ready, right Kunal?". Bidhanlooked at Ananya, searching for affirmation, "This visit has truly changed my idea of what is there in the village. It is a treasure house of peace. Looking at you, there is peace with practice. If I am here Kunal, I wont rust. I cure people in Kolkata, I will do that here. And if people are there, ailments are there, and if ailments are there, where is the question of rusting?" Ananyawondered, was Bidhan speaking to himself (as if trying to find an answer to some puzzle), or he was speaking to Kunal (as if wanting support for his thought process).

Bidhan continued, "Now, the question I would like to get it cleared before I leave, from where does the money come?"

Between You & Me

"Same question here" This from Ananya. Medicines, treatment is no cheap business. You need at least that much to survive, survive and continue".

"It is there, otherwise how do you think I am here all these years. Family, children, their education, comfortable living, own house has all come from here. My grandfather left a little kitty happily when he saw I chose the village over the city. That multiplies and gives me security. Noticed the box? Patients put in their contribution willingly, happily as per their ability. They understand the need for funds very well. The poorest of the poor also put in their might, seeing how indispensable this little infirmary is. I call it that, what else. The ones who are fairly well off push in many more notes than required. So minus here and a plus there, it balances and I manage. All my medical needs are fulfilled by this wooden coffer". Tripti was quiet all this time. She laughed, all turned towards her. "You know what, the villagers, often showed their gratitude by sending six eggs, someone bringing two bottle gourds, a fisherman putting down a nice 'Hilsa' (a type of fish, a big favourite with Bengalis, therefore in big demand) under the tube well, tamarind, mangoes, a 'lota' (a small pot like vessel) of milk, colcasia, drumstick." All started laughing. "You name it, they bring it. My kitchen is full of fresh vegetables. Kunal and I, two girls, what do we do with this bounty? It was becoming problem. Think and there is an answer to everything", Tripti continued "Kunal called a meeting of all villagers. They listened to him and nodded in agreement. And after that the money in the box rose". "Hey, no suspense. What did Kunal say?" "Kunal you say it, it was really your wonderful idea".

Kunal: "simple!. I told them, instead of giving me, they should sell the fruits and vegetables and whatever they get, should go to the box. They saw the point". "Too good, I am impressed" Bidhan said. Ananya: "But what happened to your home supply?"

"Why, I ask them to give me whenever I need it. They are only too glad to arrive next morning at the kitchen door and call out,'Ma, Ma' and gladly hand over whatever DaktarBabu wanted. By the way you must have already noticed and heard Tripti is the universal mother to everyone here, six years to sixty years". Something inside Bidhan was stirring all the time. At fiftyplus however much you want to ignore and forget it, it is not easy. In fact it comes back with greater force the next time.

Just as they were about to disperse and get ready for the day, a big noise and about a dozen people came running in, carrying a young man, his feet was dripping blood, the towel that bandaged the feet was soaked. They laid him on the table, his wife stood by him crying silently. Bidhan could feel the torcher she was going through, unable to do anything for her husband, just standing and shedding tears. Bidhan suddenly felt the air of emergency and challenge. Noise, confusion, all of them wanted to do their bit for the wounded man. Kunal ordered them out. Like meek cattle they filed out and sat down, waiting to jump at any orders given by DaktarBabu. They were readying the date palm tree for 'Khejurgur' (Date palm jaggery, a winter delicacy eagerly waited for by all bengalies), when the sharp 'Dao' (sickle) slipped and fell on the fellow's feet standing below. Thank God it was the feet and not the head, Bidhan thought. Inspite of being a doctor, a shiver ran down his spine. A terrible gash, wide and deep. Local anesthesia, tetanus, cleaning, stopping the blood, suturing and finally dressing. Good fifty minutes job. Bidhan being a surgeon had taken

Between You & Me

over. He saw the reverence in the villagers eyes. He saw how the worried face of the weeping wife was replaced by a small smile which said thank you. It was a great feeling for Bidhan and the first thing that he uttered after the villagers left, "This has made my holiday Kunal, this has made my holiday. I have never felt so glad before". After the short holiday, they were back. Back to their life and living. But for Bidhan, things were not the same. He often thought of Shibnibas, the muddy roads, the shaded paths, the flowing river, the old temple, the simple villagers and, and a village with just one doctor. "Let us go to Shibnibas, Ananya, we have a long weekend. This week was specially heavy, Dr Bhattacharya will take care of the nursing home".

Ananya and Bidhan were once again at Dr. Kunal's door. But there was lot of commotion at the gate. A tempo stood at the door, some fifteen sixteen men and women stood, waiting.

"Go in and relax, I will be back around two".Kunal said to Bidhan.

"Where are you going?"

"To Krishnanagar (District head quarter) Hospital, to show these patients, want to come?"

"Why not? Any way I will be sitting doing nothing at home"

"Hop in then, we will talk while we move". Kunalspoke, Bidhan heard. Looked admiringly at Kunal. Kunal slapped Bidhan on his back and said, "Bidhan, I have not done anything great, in my place you too would have done the same."

What flooredBidhan was this ---Medical cases which were complicated, which required machines and equipments for examination, for cases where Kunal needed a second opinion, he herded all of them into a tempo and took them to the town hospital. "My presence with them makes a difference. They are not ignored and they get the attention that is required. They are poor, they are illiterate, worse is, they are scared too. In this milieu of people who will listen to them? They will be shunted from room to room and at the end of the day they won't even know what is wrong with them. Today Doctors in Krishnanagar hospital also know me. So examinations are quick, diagnosis fast and I have a clear idea about what is to be done next. I can start off with the next line of treatment. Kunal along with Bidhan got everything done, in fact it was faster being two of them. "It was such a relief having you Bidhan, Some times taking crucial decisions all alone is very painful".

"It was a different experience altogether for me too". SpokeBidhan. "One can do things if one really wants too. I mean the difficult things".

Bidhan, back in Kunal's house, shared everything with Ananya. Ananya noticed the enthusiasm, the exhilaration in her husband. She noticed the slow and creeping change, but kept quiet. Frequency of such visits increased. While Bidhan looked forward to the change and challenge, Kunal looked forward to the company and help. Middle of the night a case of snake bite, Cases of fits or severe asthma attack, mal- nourished children, expecting mothers, dehydration, chronic stomach problems, health problems associated with old age and many more. Bidhan in his recurring visits saw them all and treated them too. Villagers now recognized him, showed happiness at his presence and simple and uncomplicated as they are, often asked him when he would come there permanently. The younger and the out spoken ones would comment "Now Kaka, who would like to leave the comforts of a city and settle in a village. Then,

DaktarBabu has his own hospital also". Such queries and comments lingered in his mind long afterwards for days to come. The debate that went on in his subconscious would suddenly surface and loom large in front of him.

Questions flitted across his mind. Pertinent questions. Troubling questions. Doubtful questions. Long and short term questions. He realized, all the questions were pertaining to him and this small obscure village called Shibnibas. One day, a young lady was rushed in with severe abdominal pain. It was unbearable, she was writhing in pain. What was more unbearable and painful was her two children, six and nine years of age howling and asking, 'Mago (ma in Bengali) you won't die no? O ma, Ma re you won't die no?'. It was a pathetic sight. Bidhan felt miserable. He did not know whether the cause of his misery was the mother or the helpless children or the silent confused father or all of them. His question was, what fate would have awaited these two little ones had there been no DrKunal. Bidhan'squestion was how many villages had how many Dr. Kunals.

When he saw Tripti helping people with physiotherapy, he wondered if people there knew, what is physiotherapy. How many can say, how it helps. He was sure, most of them were ignorant about how it is an essential part of many treatments. How it makes the difference between a wheel chair and an ambulant man.

At the beginning Triptiwas called "Kasratdaktar" Exercise doctor. Nobody came, because you get well with medicines, how can kasrat help?. That was the idea. Few, who knew about physiotherapy came, but they were few and far between. Then the comment was, 'poor Daktar's wife she has no company, she feels lonely, so few of them go to chat and give her company'. "So, how did your fortune change?" askedAnanya, turning the roti. "That is another story", Tripti said, laying the plates on the table.

"Wait then, tell it during dinner for Bidhan to hear and I am sure that is going to be one another interesting as well as entertaining story". At the dining table "Tripti, startoff your story 'Name and fame of physiotherapy in the village of Shibnibas". Tripti smiled. She recalled, "Saw the house at the end of the road? You can see it from the verandah, the one with tiled roof? well, there came this sweet, fairly fair, young Bengal beauty as a new bride to the house. After a few months, while getting a bucket full of water from the 'kalpaar' tap site, she was flat on her back, result of moss and slush. A fractured leg. Kunal did quite a bit of running after her. And why not, such a pretty thing". All burst out laughing.

"The next fracture I am attending, Kunal you keep off".

"All yours, Dr. Bidhan. The next fracture will be Bose's eighty five year old grandmother".

Tripti began "Six weeks of plaster, total bed rest. When the plaster was removed, she was limping, one day, one week, one month almost, the pain and the limp both remained. That is when 'village ki murgi' Dr.Tripti was remembered. Two months of physiotherapy and she was fit to climb a tree. And like Dr.Bidhan, I too, Dr. Tripti became famous". Tripti made a gesture of pulling up her collar.

Everything needs time in a village. Be it girls education or be it widow remarriage. Be it going out for a living. Be it getting rid of a superstition or be it Physiotherapy.

The bond between both families strengthened. Bidhan now brought the supply of medicines, every time he came. Both discussed cases, decided the line of treatment, took charge and worked together. Two and a half years passed like this... Today, while leaning back and reminiscing about Shibnibas days and remembering the 'jelly fish' incident, it dawned on him, his son was already a doctor, now in the last lap of post graduation, very soon he can hand over the reigns of his nursing home to his son, not to forget his capable second in command Dr Bhattacharya. He realized, it was the hospital that was holding him back.

Today at 2 o 'clock, when no patients waited for their turn, his mind was made. Today, just now he felt good. He felt light. He felt as if a burden is off his shoulder. He felt, he got the answer for which he was waiting all this while. He felt happy. Today was a day of extreme happiness, an indescribable satisfaction. Today his father's word meant even more. Today, he knew, at fifty five he would realize what his father dreamt of. Today the words 'It makes a difference to this one' sank in. Today he knew, he was going to Shibnibas, for the people of Shibnibas, yes, but more for himself. His decision to be there will make a difference to this village.

He got up. He needed to go to Ananya, be with her. Share, tell. In the car he was framing and reframing sentences to break the news to Ananya.

The gate opened. Ananya peered from behind the curtains. 'whocan it be? Bidhan! Back early?'. She saw him smiling, she noticed the lightness in his steps, there were no lines on his forehead. She opened the door before he rang the bell – "Ananya ----",

"Should I start packing Bidhan?"

He held her close, shut his eyes and lifted his face heaven wards.

Mummy Sunny Samvad

In Mahabharat we had the Shri Krishna -Arjun samvad. Core of the epic. In today's life too we have a core, it is the Mummy – sunny samvad. It is not a war but a confrontation between mother and son, little short of the great epic.

Fathers are lucky creatures. Being that important species called 'bread winner'they have a special place. They cannot be disturbed with electricity bill and phone bill, leaking roofs and taps, truant servants and noisy neighbours, interfering relatives etc, etc, etc.

Applies to sunny also. Average marks, long hair, torn jeans, long hours of sleep, shabby room, toomuch of internet, magnetic attraction to the mobile ---please, please don't bother the father with such mundane problems. Shouldn't the mother be managing allthis?

So, all the onus of making a hard-to manage adolescent into a decent, well-mannered boy with creditable marks falls on the mother. In the course of the day, in 18 hours (with 6 hours of sleep) several verbal altercations take place between the mother and the son. Arguments for and against will beat any court in existence. Discussions will revolve around 'Her-time' and 'His-time'.While she will uphold everything that existed during her growing years, he will bring it down like a house of cards. She will try to teach him and he will prove to be the most difficult student. At other times, he will try to put forward his point of view and the mother will be like a stone wall. The duet or is it the dual –will continue throughout the day till both of them hit the bed exhausted and exasperated. The next day they will start afresh.

But in this daily activity of preaching by one and ignoring by the other, a lot of facts surface. Note them. Enjoythem. That much discussed term 'generation –gap' comes alive in these exchanges between mother and son.

MORNING

Mummy:"Sunny get up, 5.30 already. You have a physics class at 6. You know it takes time to get ready. You know you have to reach in time as the doors of the class close at sharp 6.05. When we were young, so many brothers, sisters, cousins together still time meant time. Everybody got promptly ready and were always punctual. I repeat ALWAYS. And you people push it till the end, then rush for your class sans breakfast, at times pen or book or note book is forgotten. It will happen, it always happens when you are in a hurry and top of it disorganized".

Sunny: "Oh Ma! There you begin. Open my eyes and there you go off. In- my- time- this and in- my- time-that. Tell me Ma, did you all have tuitions that time? Was there so much of competition for seats? Were your parents nagging all the time 'study or else for 0.1 percent you may lose your seat in a coveted institution'. When was your school? At 9.30. You all got up at 8 and got ready. When do I get up?5.30 Ma 5.30. Five days in a week. Then and now there is a lot of difference Ma. Please understand".

"Okay, Okay. Now have a quick bath and get ready. My mother used to say amorning bath keeps you fresh and cool. It increases your ability to learn. All of us enjoyed our morning dip".

"Not necessarily Ma. Morning bath then under the fan of the tuition class, it makes you so sleepy. Understanding is out of question, words don't reach your ears and eyes only see a hazy board with scribblings"

"What we didn't do those days was, argue. What ever I say, you have a counter point".

"We are not argumentative Ma, but at every step we have to prove our point. We have a mind of our own. We do not like to be blind followers like your time. Days have changed. Routine, activities, pattern of study everything has changed. But will your generation accept that? NO. You will go on about your time and your days which were IDEALISTIC. But Ma remember, idealistic for you, and people of your time. Please understand we are different. We are not you. Idealistic then, may not, I say, may not be idealistic now".

"Now you will say Ma is like a broken record. But, you know what, those days there used to be one large scale breakfast of parathas or upma or poha, that is all. We used to have our fill and be happy. No complaints. Today, one day kellogs, another day sandwiches, third day egg and bread so on. One day there is a repeat and your faces pucker up as if I am serving the same thing for the last ten years. On top of it, what you like, your sister will refuse. If sister is happy with something, you will not even touch it with a barge pole. Tell me, were we bad? That adjustment was there in us. Not like now. Everything has to be tailored as per your needs and as per your likes. A selfish generation I tell you".

"Ma, let's not get into a fight. You are a fine ma and I am a fine son but why do we have to get under each other's skin through comparison. You were good. We are better. Now bye, I am off to my tuitions".

"Don't forget your stuff. We arranged our bags and books at night itself. We never forgot anything. Ask and there it would be".

"I come back from my second round of tuitions at 8.30 night, dinner, a little TV and then study. Sleep at 1, 1.30. Where is the energy to look into next day'sarrangement. Anyway you won't understand. We are running all the time. This generation lacks time, which you had in plenty. Your next sentence I will tell it for you 'and sunny we never got angry so quickly'. Fine Ma, you are the best".

EXIT

So in the morning this little Mahabharat and the generation difference.

AFTERNOON There is peace. Ma watches TV and then has her afternoon siesta. Sunny is busy in school, lecture I to lecture VIII.

Ma thinks:--When he is back from school, I must remind him to clear up his room. I wonder how he finds anything there. The study table is like a pasti bazaar. Idare not say anything. But today- he has to clear up.

Sunny thinks:- Chemistry maa'm is all animated and explaining with full gusto chemistry and all those bondings. why don't I have any bonding with chemistry. Magnetism in physics has failed to attract me anyday. Not that I am bad, but so much of overdose kills me. Chemistry here, Chemistry in the tuitions, Chemistry test and then father will say "you know, chemistry for me was like—'this', clicking his fingers, never less than 95, that is how IIT gates opened for me". 'Today Ma will definitely want me to tidy my room. Nice of her, didn't say a word past two weeks. I will do it today.

More over, those assignments of maths, I need to find. So, as well Iclean the room and see if the assignments are there anywhere in the debris.

Ding –Dong Ding –Dong Ding –Dong Ding -Dong

"Hold on. I am not getting any younger. Ha! what noise".

Sunny, mimicking ma, "Yes, in our times we entered the house as noiselessly as possible. Grandpa would be there in the entrance room having his afternoon nap. So Mamma, I saved you the trouble of repeating once again the much mouthed dialogue. In our nuclear families no grand parents, no old uncles and aunts ---so? Ring RingRingRingRing the bell".

Ma thinks ---Here we go again. Doesn't take a second and we start off like racing horses.

"your room–"

"I knew that was the agenda you planned for today".

"Don't be mean. You make me sound like a prosecutionist".

"Nice word Ma. Prosecutionist. I kind of like it. You didn't go about arranging my stuff, did you? Otherwise half the things you will throw and the other half will be missing".

"Of course I didn't touch a thing. I won't also. I wouldn't know where to begin. The bed is full of clothes. Yesterday's, day before Yesterday's, previous week and todays will be added. Study table is like a QutubMinar of books, waiting to fall at the slightest breeze. Look at the wash room. All the caps open, 'shampoo, shaving cream'".

"When we were small, each of us had a shelf and in it were all our belongings. No rooms, mind you. You all have whole rooms to yourself and you people can turn it into a small garbage can".

"Ma, you insist bathe, change, change in the evening, change at night. You know jeans are to be worn and slept in. Just think how clean my room would be. A pair of jeans and a T –shirt for the whole week. The thought itself makes me ecstatic. How! How! Very peaceful. You will peep into a clean room and I will have no cleaning up to do. Allow that Ma and see how our Mahabharat will be reduced to half".

"And study table? You had six books for six subjects. We also have six subjects. But books and notebooks galore. School, tuition, homework, classwork, tests, assignments, books for FIITJEE, AIPMT. You name it, we have it. Tables are the same size, but study material has increased six fold".

Ma comes to the point. "Today is Wednesday. So, it is Maths. Practice. More the practice, better will be the marks in Maths".

"Correct Ma. God said, He is going to increase the day by 4 more hours. If that happens Ma those 4 hours I will devote to Maths. Pucca. Baba only made the timetable –back to back. He forgot I am his son. He thought, he was planning for a robot. Can I say anything? NO. It is all for 'MY GOOD'. Bye Ma, we will keep the next episode for the night".

Ma thinks - Are all children like this? Or is it only him. I must ring Anita and find out if her son is doing the same. Deva! how much more to worry!

NIGHT 9.00 PM

Enter sunny. Bag dumped on the sofa. Shoes on the carpet. Remote in hand. Big Boss on the TVscreen.

9.45 PM

"Come, have your dinner. You have a physics test tomorrow or have you forgotten?"

"You won't let me forget. Drumstick? Rice? No chappatis? Okay, okay, like your times, I will eat without a word".

"Yes. Eat a full stomach. Kids these days, if they don't like, what is on the table, suddenly- they are not hungry any more. That is because, you all eat out so much Pav-bhaji, vada –pav, of all things Raju bhai'somlette. What is so special about it, The same omlette, you refuse at home".

"After tuitions -jabardast hunger".

"We also became ravenous, but it was always home food".

"Where was the temptation those days. No food joints at every corner. Only thing available was raw mangoes and tamarinds on the trees. No wonder you all rushed home".

"you have an answer for everything".

"And you have a comparison for everything. I need some cash".

"Cash? Monday I gave you 200 rupees. You all spend too much. Why eat out so frequently".

"The other day you said the older generation studied under street lamps. Ma, is it my fault if we have electricity today. There are lots and lots of things that we have and we need at present. You know, what my greatest fault is? Being born in this generation. I should have been a pre independence child".

"Now what? TV or the NET"

"Is this the last barb of the day, my dear mateshwari? Should I be a part of today's world or make myself mentally challenged by ignoring all the modern day gadgets?"

Ma decides to change the topic before it goes out of hand.

"TodayDikshit uncle and aunty came in the evening"

"What was the conversation? How am I fairing?.Which exams I am appearing for? Which are my coaching classes? Next – How brilliant Mr Saxena's son is!!!. How the year before last Mr Bannerjee's daughter topped. This is where I liked your generation Ma. Visitors, relatives blessed and over. No comparisons and enquiries like now. See Ma how I love people of your time".

Sunny moves to his room. Bang, the door slams.

12.30 AM

Light seeps from the bottom of the door of sunny's room. Ma decides to snoop. Walks in with a glass of milk. Sees sunny writing a birthday card. Opens her mouth –shuts it.. It is too late to begin another episode. She exits. The stiff back shows the displeasure.

Sunny thinks –Shit! Shit! Shit! All the time I studied nobody entered. Just picked up the card and there was Ma with that 'I--Knew –it' look on her face. Go to hell, Go to hell every body. True the present generation swore. Ma's time, no one swore. The twain shall meet? Or never".

WEE HOURS OF THE MORNING 4 AM, may be 4.30 AM.

Enter grand ma (Shilpa's late mother. shilpa is sunny's Ma)

Grandma: Shilpa! Shilpa! Are you asleep.

Ma: "Mummy ji you! Here? It is twelve years that you have gone. What is the matter?"

Grandma: "I am very perturbed".

Ma: "Why?"

Grandma: "Look at the way you and your son are at loggerheads. All day. Every day".

Ma: "You saw no Mummy ji how he argues. How he behaves".

Grandma: "Only he argues? Only his behavior is bad?"

Ma:" What do you mean? Your tone suggests even I am at fault".

Grandma: "No one is at fault. It is the generation gap. Face it, accept it. It was there yesterday, it will be there tomorrow and today you are going through it".

Ma: "Out with it mummy ji. You didn't reappear just for this small speech".

Grandma: "Saw, you are speaking just like sunny, ready to blow your top. Remember, how you sat on the corner sofa and nagged and nagged about the outstation trip, till your father said yes, and I walked out in a huff. Girls didn't go out for overnight trips those days. It was not the done thing. Was there not a difference between what you wanted and what we thought".

Ma opens her mouth to speak. "Stop. I have not finished yet. Did you not insist on going out with your husband atleast once or twice before the alliance was finalised. Was that not diverting from the regular code of conduct. What was your reply? I still remember 'Mummyji this is how it is in the present generation'".

Grandma continues. "I am not over yet. Don't forget your wearing bell pants. Not to mention the short tops. Did we not accept it allowing the word 'modern' to take care of the arising problems".

"And right now? Where are you wearing saris, apart from formal occassions. Ninety nine percent of the time you are in, what you call them, leggings and kurtis. So don't be sarcastic about his choice of clothes".

"Amount of money you spend on crockery, home décor, cosmetics, entertainment and you keep count of Rs 200 that you give that poor son of yours. Badiammi used to stand on all you children's head to clear the mess. You happily forgot those days? I think these many examples are enough for you. So, see, feel, understand your son, see his point of view, his difficulties, his needs. Make him happy".

Before Shilpa could speak, she disappeared. Leaving her words behind her.

It was early morning. Ma sat on the bed, mummyji and what she said floated in the room. The alarm went off jarringly bringing her back to the present. Bringing her back to the needs of the day –milk, breakfast, tiffin. But other things remaining the same, today was not the same.

She got up, straightened and stretched. Softly she opened the door to her sons bed room. There he was fast asleep with books all around him. Things all around – from leather jacket to laptop. No it won't be like other days. She sat in the curve created by his sleeping body. She caressed his hair. She ran her hand over his back. She could feel his ribs. Is he losing weight, studying and running from class to class. A soft breeze wafted through his straight hair. She said goodbye to the nagging, shouting days.

"Sunny, get up. Time for tuitions"

"Yes Ma. Five more minutes. Just, Five minutes", and he put his arms around her waist." Ma you are the worlds bestestMa" She ruffled his hair. He didn't see her misty eyes.

She got up. Proceeded to the kitchen for yet another day. She could hear him getting ready. He had his breakfast, downed his glass of milk, picked up his things, gave her a tight hug and left.

Was it the same house? Were the people same? So peaceful. Where was the hassle, the hurry, not to mention the hard words. Truly, every generation is new, their thinking new, their ideas new, their maturity new. We have to take it in our stride and mould accordingly. When we change and accept, they will learn from us to change and accept in return. Life will be an amalgam and not a constant conflict.

She sat down at the dining table with her cup of tea. In a contemplating mood. Lost in her own thoughts. The steaming cup pepped her, but like other days, there was not a dire need for it.

She looked up. She looked around. Expecting mummyji to come before her. She opened her eyes. Yesterdays generation taught the current generation what to do for the coming generation. She gave the two key words UNDERSTAND and ADAPT. Thank you mummyji. Thank you for the 'THE END' of Mahabharat.

Return of Ipshita

Surjo, while driving, for the nth time felt, he should have been more assertive. But he was not made that way. He knew that too. In good faith he always put forward his view, his solutions to office problems but he was not made to fight for them ferociously and insist on their acceptance. Old and well meaning colleagues often advised him to be adamant in his approach, should not let go so easily. It was discussed in the office that, in today's corporate world till you throw a few cuss words chances of being accepted is less. Some went a step forward and added 'more the cuss words faster is the climb on the official ladder'. Who knows. For him, he cannot be what he is not. But this 'to be' or 'not to be' often irritated him. He could not push away the day's happening and say 'forget it'.

In this frame of mind, he reached home and opened the gate. The garden lay unwatered. Many of the delicate plants had their leaves drooping. Was he like these plants? He did not like the answer that passed his mind.

The drawing room door was open. The fan on, in full speed. The news paper, half of it fluttering under the sofa and the other half was in an athletic position to 'get set and go'. Two tea mugs with remnants of tea turned black lay on the centre table, yet to be removed. The single sofas looked 'sat in' but not straightened after wards. Nothing new, such scenes welcome him every day.

He walked to the kitchen, hoping to find something for his hungry stomach. The kitchen looked unnaturally clean, spic and span, showing, the kitchen had a holiday. His hope of finding something to eat vanished into thin air. This also was a regular occurrence.

His steps took him to the bedroom. There she was, holding her hands faraway for the nail enamel to dry and at the same time admiring her fair beautiful hands, now even more beautiful with the new colour.

"Oh you are here! Didn't hear you" said his stunningly beautiful wife, Suparna.

"Why everything is in such a disarray. what is the occasion for having a 'no cooking' day?"

"Oh, the fan and all. I suddenly got up to decide what I should wear for the evening and rushed to the bedroom. Today is the monthly dinner at theclub, so no cooking. You forgot?"

"How can I? This is the day I get to eat everything, soup to sweet, not forgetting the other things in between".

"How mean! Don't talk like this". She got up and turned around to show her new embroidered blouse. It had less of material and showedmore of her lovely fair skin. Her black silky hair flowed down to her waist. "You like this colour? It is one of the new colours from the Revlon range", showing a set of white pearly teeth she smiled, satisfied with her nails and the blouse, which she was scrutinizing from all angles. "Don't you worry, you will be the prettiest woman in the whole crowd, your day will be made".

She knitted her brows, "Something happened in the office? You! upset? Share with me". Share!, as if she was interested, in ten seconds she will go back to her looks and attire. Some onesaid, 'beauty is skin deep', that person did not meet Suparna. Her beauty obsession goes upto the marrows. Nothing less.

"I will be wearing my plain chiffon with the printed border, that is an unusual combination. Surjo, do you think I wore it before? Else where?"

How these questions used to be so important after marriage. In 730 days of marriage, all his interest has evaporated. So far he has failed to communicate and assert that with looking ravishing there also should be some good cooking, good housekeeping, good entertaining and atleast some good conversation other than beauty, beauty tips, beauty accessories, beauty shopping and ……………oh how he despised the word beauty. Of course he will be silent about it. Pick up a fight? That is the last thing he wanted, anytime, any where. He was always like this. He disliked confrontations, arguments. Good or bad, he preferred his ways. Not hurling painful word is much better than being assertive.

"Get ready Surjo, we will be meeting two new couples Mr. and Mrs. Vinay Sharma and Mr. and Mrs. Debojeet Sinha. You have of course met the men, the women will be new to you, I will meet all of them for the first time".

"Suparna, not to worry, you will floor all of them".

"Don't be sarcastic I dress for you too".

"Yes, me too, not me only".

"What ever your intentions, I take it positively. You are so very possessive about your wife. I am not going to worry unnecessarily about your comments and get untimely lines on my forehead".

Surjo looked at her. Surprise written all over his face. What a lady! She ran, came to him, kept her newly painted nails at a safe distance, kept her sari intact, and gave a peck on his cheek. Now she will apply her lipcolour. How well he knew her.

They set off for the party. From a distance they saw the well lighted club house. Conversation floated out in a suppressed manner from behind the closed door and heavily curtained windows.

They stepped in and conversation stopped for fleeting seconds while every body took in the picture perfect Mr. and Mrs. Surjo Roy. Suparna smiled, looking even more pretty as both proceeded towards the gathered crowd.

Hi and Hellos ensued, then it was Prashant Mittal "come here yaar, meet the new ladies, call Suparna, let's finish with the introduction.

"Suparna" Surjocalled out.

Mittal eager to introduce,"Vinay and Debjeet, here with your wives".

"This is Sushma that is Mrs. Sharma and here is another beauty from Bengal for you Ipshita, Ipshita Sinha".

"Ipshita, You!!! of all the places, in the officers club of ALCO in Raigarh".

"Surjo, am I happy to see you? How you got lost so suddenly, no touch, what so ever. Don't smile that usual smile, I am not going to forgive you".

"Ipshita, forgiving comes naturally to you, you were so popular in Ghatshila among all the aunts uncles and grandmas, not to forget the teenagers with their 'Ipshita di, Ipshita di' revolving around you".

"So much to talk - Surjo, you and Suparna come over for dinner, so much to share and exchange. Debjeet this is The Surjo, I talked of so often. He is the same, that shy smile, waiting for his chance to say something".

"When will you come overSurjo? Ipshita would enjoy talking to you, six years Ipshita? Or is it five?"

"I Don't know Deb, it just seems yesterday". "True, I still miss those days of Ghatshila. Everything is still so fresh".

They went back to the crowd.

Coming Sunday was the day. Suparna looked at her husband. He looked so happy. He was so animated. She couldn't remember him like this any time before.

Surjo thought, Just like Mashima (Ipshita's mother), Call any body and every body home without a second thought. Every body was welcome in that house hold. Ipshita'ssisters, one older and one younger too were like that. Always smiling, always welcoming. they loved to share 'gheebhath' --Bengali pulao or 'jhalmury' -- spiced puffed rice, most willingly. It was an open household which exuded love and warmth all the time. No doubt Surjo, even at the chagrin of his elder sister would run away to their house at the first opportunity. He not only looked for opportunities, he created them also. Now after so many years he felt the welcome of Ipshita's words just like old times. Suparna also would be extremely happy, one day less to cook.

Surjo enjoyed the party, he would run to Ipshita with his plate and they would get down to sharing old times.

Debjeet looked down at his wife,"You are one memory, my wife loves to cherish and share with me. Iknow quite a bit of her days in Ghatshila, your family and you specially. I am so glad we meet again".

Back home, Surjo counted four more days to Sunday." How quickly she invited us, must be the good house keeper type" said Suparna, rubbing in those expensive creams she used. "Yes they, her family love people. About housekeeping we will see on Sunday. In Ghatshila it was ordinary like any other Bengali household".

Surjo lay down, one hand across his forehead, his eyes on the ceiling.

"What happened? Don't want to sleep?" enquired Suparna.

"No. So many happy memories, buried, forgotten for so long, are just popping up one after the other".

Surjo's sister after marriage moved to Ghatshila with her husband. Surjo then was in his final year of engineering. For his semester break he rushed to his sister, loaded with all the goodies made by his mother, looking forward to a nice, cosy holiday with his newly married sister and newly acquired 'Jamaibabu'. Green Ghatshila with Subarnorekha, no more a river but a stream, the factory quarters hidden behind lush gardens, the not very distant hills, the weekly market, the simple locals were all so peaceful and soothing.

He was on his own exploring. A group of 7 to 8 girls, aged 10 to 12 came, shouting and talking. They stopped, "Are you new?"

Surjo wanted some fun, "No I am old, aged"

"Yes you are old. You can't even understand a simple question" said one of the girls.

"Let's go 'Let's go. He is acting smart".

"He is new, never seen him before".

"Which house has he come? Any idea?"

That was the introduction to the youngest one of Ipshita's household.

Surjo after reaching home "Didi, there was this bunch of girls ----". He related what happened.

"They belong to the colony, all in their high school, nice girls, evenings they are out together"

Surjo met neighbours, people known to his sister, the sabjiwala, the fish seller, every body of any consequence to his sister.

Surjo's counting days and hours was over, they were at Debjeet and Ipshita's door for the promised dinner. Suparna was dressed to kill. Peacock blue silk, sleeveless blouse with blue crystals to match.

Ipshita opened the door and commented candidly, "How beautiful you look Suparna, Surjo you lucky guy". Like old times, Surjosaw Ipshita's smile reach her eyes.

The drawing room was beautifully kept, unlike her mother's house in Ghatshila. Everything had a touch of Ipshita, the embroidery, the family photographs, Debjeet and Ipshitas snaps, the fresh flowers. Surjolooked around appreciatively.

"Nice Ipshita. A home like this every body would love to have". Debjeet made a good husband. Surjo concluded after watching him. He was a good conversationalist, laughed easily, kept helping Ipshita with plates and spoons, laying the table. Altogether a homely atmosphere that Surjowas enjoying whole heartedly. The food? It was all Surjo'sfavourite. Surjowas astonished. "Ipshita you still remember?"

"Remember?" Debjeet intervened. "I never had so much trouble shopping, everything had to be perfect to the T. Detailed instructions on things to be bought. She enjoyed cooking for youSurjo. That she is a good cook is another fact. No showing off friend, you will be left licking your fingers".

"LikeMashima then. Any time I arrived, there would be some thing for me, all so delicious".

It was an enjoyable evening. The company, the food, everything was made for each other. On returning,"Surjo, the way you ate!! It looked as if you were famine struck". "Yeah, I miss good food. When was the last time you cooked a full meal? A good meal?"

Suparna kept quiet. Why open the pandoras box. "I told you she is the good housekeeper types". "Yes the house keeper in every woman that husbands love". "If you are hinting, I am sorry, cooking is not my forte". "If you can take out time from your make up kit and your dresses, then you can think of spending some time in the kitchen. Forget about being beautiful all the time. For a change, think of dishing up something beautiful. Do that". Surjo was astonished by his own comment. Was it him speaking? Suparna too was taken aback by this unusual, sudden outburst.

Surjo slipped once again into the past. He was at Ghatshila. Semester break again.

"Today, we are invited to Mr. Sarkar's house for Lakshmi Puja. Dinnertoo---prasad and bhog". Surjo dressed in kurta – pyjama stepped into the Sarkar house hold and lo –there was one of those perky girls, whom he had confronted in one of the exploratory walks. "Hi! Remember me?" "How can I forget you friend? New or Old?" "Little old and a little new". "Right". "I am Mr. Sarkar's youngest daughter. I have two elder sisters. They are here somewhere".She vanished with her friends. Masshima arrived on the scene. "Surjo, you have come. Sit, I will call one of the girls". Surjo 's sister said, "Mashima, its okay. We will take care of ourselves". A little later, "Here is Shobita, Surjo, this is mashima's eldest daughter, the other one is Ipshita. introduce you when I see her". Surjo met Ipshita. She was serving the bhog, sari tucked in, hair in a knot sweating, but smiling away happily, a smile that reached her eyes.. Surjo liked what he saw.

"good people didi" he told his sister. "There is so much warmth in the family".

"Warmth, yes, but so ordinary, not our type".

Surjo wanted to know what 'our type'meant, then decided why bother. After all how much did he know the family, to take up cudgels on their behalf.

Between You & Me

In that holiday he met Ipshita two, three times. Twice outside and once when she pulled him to her house. When they were together conversation flowed. They could talk on anything and everything. She laughed and the sound of her laugh attracted him, no distracted him, no, no, attracted him ---whatever it is, he loved her laugh, he loved to hear her laugh. He was beginning to feel, just like him, she too liked his company. She looked forward to his visit just like he would wait to visit her home, after she returned from college.

It became a regular feature. During holidays Surjo arrived at Ghatshila. His sister complained, he spent too much time in the Sarkar household than with her. Shobhita, IpshitaSurjo enjoyed all those things that young people enjoy. Movies, eating out, shopping, chatting idly, directionless days, which flowed taking them along in its course. Every day would be replete with some plan that made sure they were together. Happy days came and went.

Break over, exams over, results also over. He got a job with one of the IT companies. He was happy that things were happening and falling into place. He rushed to Ipshita'shouse to break the news. The little sister shrieked in excitement, Mashima arrived with a plate of rosogollas from nowhere, the two elder sisters Shobhita and Ipshita were smiling from ear to ear.

He was visibly sad to leave for Kolkata, from where he would proceed to his new job. When they met, Ipshita agreed she was going to miss him. But this was expected.

Suparna broke his reverie.

"Lost in thought? About Whom?"

"Yes, I was thinking about my Ghatshila days and our friendship with ipshita's family".

"Were you very fond of her? Very fond?"

"We were good friends and loved each other's company. I went off for my job, Didi's husband took up a new assignment and I never went back to Ghatshila. The Ghatshila chapter including Ipshita closed".

Suparna felt relieved. Thanked God and proceeded towards the bedroom to select a sari for Mrs.Gohil's farewell.

Surjo did not tell Suparna that was not the last chapter, that, there was a last chapter he preferred not to disclose. A chapter which was unknown to Ipshita also.

Past is past. He got up, shook himself, stretched, walked, but he knew, by this, his thoughts cannot be shaken off. Like today and many other days before, like a gust of wind, it will barge in, disturb, upset and vanish. He will once again take time to wipe and clean old memories and get back to the present.

Good, he met her after these many years as Mrs. DebjeetSinha. That should help to erase memories of their togetherness in Ghatshila. Not erase exactly but help to take things in its proper perspective.

They, the four of them met often. Every time they visited, dinner was a must, therefore more time spent together. Suparna welcomed it too, what with readymade dinner as a bonus. But Surjo saw so much of Mashima in Ipshita, shirking work was not her way of doing things, having open house all the time was a direct inheritance. In case of Suparna and Surjo, they were family for Ipshita and Debjeet.

Ipshita would rush in, in the evening, keep a tiffin on the dining table, Suparna would open and the aroma of 'Kasha Mangsho' (fried lamb) would fill the room. She would come in with a strand of jasmine and say, "Suparna, put round your small bun, you will look lovely, and smell lovlier". Both would come over because Debjeet wanted to talk shop. A phone call would be there in the morning itself if it was one of Surjo'sfavourite dishes.

Surjo looked forward to the homeliness of her home and the bengalines of her food. Sometimes he wished for more pro activeness from his wife, but kept quiet hoping Suparna will realize herself one day, someday.

The first time Ipshita and her husband was invited, Suparna was busy planning the evening, which restaurant, what food etc. Surjo spoke strictly "we are entertaining them at home".

"At home?"

"Yes, here, at home".

"What will I Cook?"

"you decide, but it is going to be home food".

Surjo's tone told Suparna, no further argument will be entertained. She was perturbed. Too perturbed. But she knew Surjo meant every word of what he said.

"Let this house also show it is cared for, at least for the first time, later they will come to their own conclusions".

Suddenly Suparna felt very inadequate. So far she sailed through with her beauty. That was natural. Now, this was a challenge. There was nothing wrong in Surjo's demand. Suddenly she was angry. Why was he not insistent before? Then, today she would have been better equipped.

Ipshita was a dear, she came in the morning. In the evening, she came early to help Suparna out. Suparna for the first time felt the satisfaction of feeding people at home. Thanks to Surjo for his insistence and thanks to Ipshita and Debjeet for happily tolerating the less salt in the fish and the over sweetness of the kheer.

The over indulgence in looks continued, but she saw, Ipshita also looked beautiful. She could be, would be, ready in a jiffy. She too used latest fashions, expensive make up. But there were times, she would just use a hair band to keep her hair in place, may be a dash of lipstick and look good. She was not fastidious about her looks or attire.

Once Surjo and Suparna were going for a movie when Ipshita and Debjeet arrived. They decided on a four some. Ipshita applied a little powder and kajal. That's it. Suparna looked asif she has just stepped out of a fashion magazine. But who would be impressed in a dark theatre.

Days continued. Ipshita and Debjeet never knew how they were both impacting the other couple. While Surjo was taking a more stricter stance in house hold matters, Suparna was realizing her immaturity in her obsession with looks and looking good.

Why this change in Surjo after two years of marriage? Why now? He knew the answer, because the last chapter of the story, known only to him, came back more frequently now than ever.

Back to old days.

"You are going to join your new job, why are you so down cast?" asked his sister.

Surjo kept quiet.

"Why quiet?" His sister questioned again.

Surjo did not know what to say or how to say it.

His sister probed, "Don't tell me, are you upset because you are going to miss the Sarkar house hold? Rather, you will miss Ipshita in particular?"

Surjo hurried with his words, "yes didi, I like her, like her a lot. No, we haven't said those precious three words to each other, but on the threshold of my departure I realised my feelings for her run deeper".

"Forget it", his sister took up, "I told you before, they are not our type. Can you see our ma in her starched cotton sari approving Ipshita's mother's crumpled, turmeric stained sari which sees an iron once in a while".

"Didi, are such things important? Mothers are important, but what they wear and how they wear, is it crucial for a marriage? I will not be marrying the family, I am interested in Ipshita. And by the way if it helps, I like the family too".

"Don't decide by yourself and don't go prophesying your love for Ipshita, let us talk to Ma first".

Mistake. The first mistake that he committed-he agreed and kept quiet. Said bye to Ipshita and family and moved to Bombay to his new job.

His mother, on getting the details, both mother and daughter landed In Mumbai on the pretext of settling him and in the process tell him how wrong his choice is in every respect.

"Charming, yes, but she is not beautiful".

"But I like her. That much beauty is enough for me".

"Bapi (His mother's name for him) you are going to be working in Mumbai, you need a suitable partner. It is a decision for life you know".

Surjo listened.

"They were trying to hook you, and who won't. Such an eligible bachelor in every way".

Surjo objected.

"Now Ma You don't agree, that is one thing but don't malign them like this".

"Three sisters! think of the marriage expenses. can her father manage. No sons, later the son-in-laws have to take the responsibility".

"Don't you think you are thinking too much ahead of time?"

"Fine", she used the last weapon, with tear filled eyes, she said, "but promise you won't take a hasty decision and not without talking to me, promise?"[1]

Surjo nodded his head. That was his second mistake. He did not put his foot down. Left things to take its own course.

With busy Mumbai life, responsibilities, memories receded to the background. He often thought of them, thought of Ipshita but felt odd that all of a sudden after so many months he is popping back into their life. He failed to realize that it happens with many and he is no exception. His laid back attitude came in the way. When he wanted to talk, it was many months and his shame of not keeping in touch held him back. He also said to himself 'it was not love' so let her go.

Suparna walked into his life. The only child of well-to - do parents. Their style, urbane outlook and of course Suparna's beauty floored him. Surjo's family too was all for the one in a million match. They were married.

It took a couple of months for Surjo to understand Suparna's nature. But was he the person to take objection? Accepted Suparna the way she was and adjusted accordingly. Ipshita once in a while floated back into his thoughts, but he knew that was a door that was closed because of him.

Now Ipshita reappeared. A loving, caring and an understanding wife to Debjeet, whose eyes showed. how he thought the world of her. Their compatibility was evident to whoever met and saw them. Surjo felt happy for them. He still loved Ipshita that much, to wish them happiness and know they deserved each other. Ipshita was the long lost friend and Debjeet was the newly found friend via Ipshita. Surjo's loss was Debjeet's gain.

He got up. "Suparna, Suparna".

"Here I am. Drying my hair"

"Which get – together is it now?".

"Tomorrow, Ladies club".

"Fine, finish drying and get the dinner ready. I am hungry"

"Surjo" 'With that tone dripping love', Suparna used to get things done, "We have some bread, get some chicken from lucky restaurant".

"No chance. Get up and dish out something. I will wait. I am not going anywhere".

"Su—r---Jo -----"

"I am deaf".

Next day. "How was your kitty party?"

"Gorgeous!. Everybody admired my Chanderisari. (Shyly) The colour compliments my skin you know".

Good. Make something for me, you won't be hungry I know. Also, before I forget, when it is your turn, prepare everything at home, no outside food …strictly".

The beautiful Suparna was aghast. Was it Surjo speaking?

"Take Ipshita's help if you need. Though I think, you should do it on your own".

Days passed. Suparna missed the earlier Surjo. She was dusting the rooms. The 'okay, fine, will do' husband of hers was now politely stubborn, quite adamant and stuck to his guns. What he wanted, the way he wanted, had to be done. Suparna in her heart of heart knew, what he was demanding today, that she should have done long ago. Is he demanding or has she woken up to her wifely duties albeit after being pushed. Whatever, coming back to present realities, it is high time she thawed the fish. Gone are those days when Lucky restaurant was their dinner supplier majority of the days. She also better remember that the Kapoors are coming over this weekend. Oh God! Oh God!.She sprang back to her feet. Gone are those days when her feet were permanently on the table or stool.

The phone rang, "Suparna, me, Surjo. Please ready the house, I am getting guests. Make sure some snacks are there". He hung up. Suparna stared back at her mobile.

After the guests left, "Surjo", she stopped him, holding his arm, "What happened? You are ordering me about. You realize that?"

"No, not ordering, only telling my lovely wife, things to be done. Two years of marriage over? Good time to hold the bull by the horns".

"What? I am a bull? I really don't understand you these days".

"Call you a bull? No bodydares to do that my pretty wife. You don't understand me? How can you? I am beginning to understand myself only now"

"What is it Surjo? Not another puzzle?"

"Forget it". The exasperated look on Suparna'sface, he felt bad for Suparna, but he consoled himself with the thought that she will eventually understand.

One day, "There is a nice movie in town, get ready in a jiffy. Either you are out with me or you stay back. Don't start your beauty parlour regime". Needless to say, Suparna was in the car before he could honk. Suparna realized, actually this was good too."Here Surjo, Mothers Call. Your mother"

Whatever was said on the other side, Suparna had no idea, but she was astonished to hear Surjo speak like this,

Between You & Me

of all people, to his mother, who all the time nodded his agreement. He was saying "No, No Ma, not possible, don't expect us to go to Nagpur to mashis (aunts) place. Yes, I will definitely go but as per my comfort and convenience".

Suparna walked towards her bedroom and thought, this was an usual conversation between any mother and son, but between Ma and Surjo, a surprise, because so far this was not usual but quite unusual.

Surjo's change permeated into his office too.

"Sir" His subordinate was beaming, "That was the correct stance, sir. You put them in their place. Now, we can do the things our way". Suparna thought and her heart swelled with pride, when she overheard the men's conversation, where Mr Rastogi was all praise for Surjo for being bold and sticking to his plan and policy.

Suparna was not dumb. She analysed, brooded, to figure out what triggered the change. Instances, incidents, occurrences, situations showed the metamorphosis in Surjo.

Suparna, now, managed house with beauty. His mother could not boss. His sister was ready for opposition. Office never took him for granted. No meek, not meek rather polite submission like before. It took the loss of Ipshita and the return of Ipshita to make him realize what was wrong with him and how to make it right.

Two Women in My Life

Two women in my life. One, who made me twenty two years of age & the other, who took me over at twenty two. One, my mother & the other, my mother -in-law. The trust begins when an infant (few hours old) snuggles up to the mothers bosom for the warmth and care. The trust begins then & continues in memory, even when the mother is a twinkling star in the inky blue sky. The mother-in-law holds your hand & leads you in & that continues even when you yourself are a mother-in-law. Compliments come your way –about your intelligence, your scores, your good sense of humour, your good house-keeping, but behind the scene, is the patient mother who teaches you to first hold the pencil and then burns her heart & soul with your midnight oil. In every thing you do, there is your mother's gentle touch.

Your mother -in-law will initiate you into the slippery world of running a household, comprising of even more slippery members & most slippery finances. When we have our own greying hair, failing eyesight and tired limbs, we can't thank them enough for being what they were.

My mother's fragrance still floats around me. My mother-in-laws eyes still follow me around.

I am that lucky species where the mother & the mother -in-law got along like 'a house on fire'. They planned together, came together, stayed together, helped and harassed (truly) together and tearfully left together.

Once in the train they were asked, "Mashima (aunt in Bengali) Where are you both going?"

Ma, "To Baroda".

Mother -in-law, "To Baroda"

"Where in Baroda, Mashima?"

Ma, "To my daughter's house."

Mother -in-law "To my son's house".

After a few hours --- "Mashima, which place in Baroda?"

Ma, "Manjalpur". Mother -in-law, "Manjalpur".

After the co-passenger heard all their yapping with all the gossip, this ones nephew, so and so's son, good and bad servants and the rest -----it was becoming too, too puzzling.

"Mashima, you both know each other well, isn't it?"

The duo with plain faces, "Yes, extremely well".

"Give both your address. I will try and pay both of you a visit".

The lovely ladies, Ma and Mother -in-law handed over the address. The lady read it once, twice. Looked at both of them, properly surprised, confused, puzzled. "You both have the same address? You live in the same house?"

Ma and Mother -in-law, "Yes". Then they thought enough and decided to end the suspense. Ma "you see, my daughter is married to her son".

Mother -in-law, "Yes, her daughter is my daughter -in-law".

Now you know, how they are such writable material. Absolutely crazy. But adoringly crazy, I would add.

With me, they had their days filled with bantering, sharing, chiding, working together.

Ma, "Today you cook".

Mother -in-law, "of course not. You cook cabbage well. I want to eat cabbage cooked by you".

Ma, "What else to do? Your son's house, I am at your mercy".

Mother -in-law, "I always knew one big drama queen you are".

Another day. Ma, "What are you doing sitting with that heap of clothes?"

Mother -in-law, "All repair work, poor thing, where is the time for her".

Ma, "Good. Sometimes you are a good mother -in-law".

Mother -in-law, "Of course, Are you a good mother -in-law?"

Ma, "Ah ha, ask my son-in law".

At other times -- mother -in-law, "Don't work so much and fall sick. Sikha will do it"

Ma, "Sit and rest. You have done enough for the day".

Their days would be filled like this and my heart would swell with pride when I came back from work and saw them sitting in their favorite chairs, watching their favorite Bengali serial.

I can't forget their shopping spree.

First declaration: "We both are pensioners. Take us there, where the stuff is good and the prices are cheap".

Once there, the two get engrossed like little children. Touch this, feel that, ask the price, move on, come back. After they have shopped for relatives, friends, pujari ji, maid at home and numerous others, then Second declaration.

"We will come another day. It is a good place, Bouma (bahu in Bengali) bring us here again". After that, they loved to decide the snacks both will buy to take home and have that large glass of tea –U.P style. (Mother -in-law was in Kanpur for a long period of time).

When with us, we always took them out to some special place for dinner. At first both would wail,"No, no, don't waste your money. Let us have idli, dosa". This they approved, light on the purse but heavy in the stomach. But of course we never listened to them. Once in the eating place, they enjoyed and admired the ambience, the décor, the food and even the cutlery, the napkins and looked so thankful. We would say, you gifted us the ability to treat you like this, we should thank you instead.

Invariably a 'tirth yatra' was a part of the package. We also used the bait to its fullest. Ambaji, Shrinath ji, Dwarka, Somnath, Dakor were visited. If they were ecstatic, we were more ecstatic seeing their faces. Faces of bhakti, satisfaction, happiness. Every thing culminated on their blessings on us. Children are always the gainers – this way or that.

In Calcutta they would visit each other. Plan temple visits. Carry cooked food. Remind each other about their doctor's check up. When my father passed away, my mother in law was a tower of strength for all of us. Constantly by my mother's side, she reduced her pain and anguish. When my father in law was no more, my mother rushed to her every day.

Such good friends, such good relation, such good luck, we had them. Today as a mother in law myself, much of my actions are prompted and guided by them. You do follow footsteps, don' you? I wish every household is blessed by such foot steps.

One day Asim (my husband) tells me "What if our mothers were not like this?"

Me, "What is NOT LIKE THIS?"

He, "Like being such good friends, caring for each other, sharing………"

Me, "So?"

He, "So our house would be one arena for a new 'Mahabharat'. Ma and daughter versus son and mother".

We burst out laughing, thanking GOD for the TWO WONDERFUL WOMEN in our lives.

By the way, I should actually change the title to 'Four women in my life'. The new entrants being my daughter and my brand new daughter in law.

Workshop!!!

Wow! A workshop. Too good yaar!! You will not find people welcoming a workshop like this.

The only person who is truly thrilled about it is your BOSS. That day he walks into the office breezily, adjusts his tie & pulls his coat closer to his prosperous tummy, stands in the middle of the room, under the fan, looks around (which says what a lucky bunch you all are) and announce,

"There will be a workshop tomorrow, from 3 - 7 PM". (don't miss the stress on 3 - 7 PM) While you all are still sitting, rising & in standing position he will walk out with his smartest gait, repeating "3 - 7, remember", Which means, you all better be present even if it is a Saturday.

Now about the workshop. They all have long, highly intellectual, technical, important sounding names. 'Vibration analysis of the transmission gear of a small car'(don't try to understand, you already know it).

'Education –yesterday, today & tomorrow, in context of gurukul & liberal education'(Careful! More the time span, longer will be the workshop), 'Paradigm Shift in education'(What is that? –Now, don't show your ignorance.) Even the most well informed, most learned in your office will have his forehead wrinkled & his eyes screwed. But that is okay. What is that workshop which doesn't have an awe inspiring title.

Next comes the speaker. Some come absolutely formally dressed coat, suit, tie et al. They will walk briskly, talk swiftly, walk up & down, left & right & you can be sure, you will not fall asleep. Because all the time you are trying to keep pace with the speaker. The other type is the jean clad, stiff formal white shirt types with some accent thrown in. He will walk, talk, stop, look, & careful, questions you suddenly.

There are those in 'Rin White' kurta –pyjama & a light coloured striped khadi jacket—may be or may be not. They will intersperse their delivery with Hindi, Sanskrit & shayri.

Coming to the talk. Some are so serious, so serious, you feel they are Hercules carrying the atlas. The topic is highly intellectual, the talk even more intellectual, the listeners least intellectual. Result – Every body is looking at their watch & wandering if it is showing the right time.

Some speakers or is it few? They are good. Beautifully tailored material which is easily graspable. Difficult stuff made easy. New stuff wonderfully communicated. Sprinkling of humour. Life examples. And there are lots of nods & smiles among the audience.

Humour. Some speakers are so humourless as if humour is a sin. Others have an overdose of humour, so much so, the participants wonder if they are watching 'comedy nights with Kapil'. While others humour the public. The speaker has a quirk on his face, a raised eyebrow & a challenging look. But let me not be too cynical. We do have these speakers with a wonderful sense of humour accompanied with very relevant anecdotes, appropriate body language, that is when the audience have an appreciative look and all are actually participating.

The best part – right, it is the lunch. If it is a corporate office or a prestigious institution, you have a great spread, soup -------dessert ----- veg and non-veg. Have you noticed, people then eat double the amount? No, they are not gluttons. It is the boredom. Have you not read in the magazines which says you add weight when you binge more due to boredom. I think there is some truth in it.

After lunch it is the most difficult time. It is that tremendous effort that you are making to keep your eyes open & look attentive at the same time. You wait for the big respite in the form of tea & biscuit. You really thank GOD for keeping this break. Tea was never more refreshing & biscuits never more crispier.

Yes, another hour to go & every body will be home bound. A complaining wife, a demanding child, a noisy teenager, a barking dog, all seem to be God sent (compared to the almost ending or is it non ending workshop).

15 minutes to go. Close your pens, arrange your papers, lock your brief case while the speaker is winding up. The person who has to give the vote of thanks is already standing shamelessly.

Now for the icing on the cake, the resource person says ---"Now, any questions?" Oh God, how unkind can you be? Silence all around. The boss looks at everybody hintingly. "MY TEAM and no questions". One or two take the cue, think hard, & pop some face saving questions. In the audience, one tells the other, "My 7.15 local will go". Another one "yaar, I have my mother –in –law visiting me & I will be late, both the mother & daughter will take me to the slaughter house". Boss looks. All fall silent. & try to make out the answer to the question. But in vain.

And then the lucky hour, no, the lucky minute, sorry! the lucky second strikes. The invited guest gives you a beaming thank you, the bold ones walk out boldly. The new & the timid ones will lag around & exclaim "Great sir. Too good ". "Can we have your E mail Id?" Of course. What is a workshop if no future clientele is built.

When you reach home your wife never looked more beautiful & her smile even more welcoming. You even like your mother–in –law. If you are a female, after a workshop, your better half will insist on getting food from outside.

Note for the BOSSES. But the SHOW, Sorry! the workshops must go on.

To See or Not To See

The Host: TH
Maheshwari Sari: Ms.MS
Slim and Trim: Ms. S& T
Bengali Didi: Ms. BD
Delhiite: Ms D
Pattu Sari: Ms PS
Guju Ben: Ms.GB
G.M's Wife: GMW

I love kitty parties. Specially when someone else is hosting. I take out my newest chiffon/silk (as per the season). I match my accessories – If not available, a good shopping spree hunting for it with a 'good lunch' thrown in as a bonus. The latest hand bag given by my cousin in the U.S.A comes out. My nails show off the nail enamel bought last week specially for this get together. Thank you, no colossal kajal for me. I look ghastly and ghostly both. And if I win the draw nothing like it. A nice lump sum amount in my hand, which hubby will come to know but will never get, though the initial contribution comes out of his pocket.

We were all settled, eyeing each other from the corner of our eycs, noticing the glittering diamond bracelet of Ms.GMW. Surreptiously looking at the golden sandals of Ms. S and T, Debating (of course in our mind) if the new hair cut of Ms.GB was right or too much. While we were contemplating such important (truly!) matters, there walked in Ms MS.

Ms.MS: "Hi! Every body. Sorry! sorry! I am late". Looks at her watch, "by 20 minutes. Can't miss my serial".

Ms. S and T: "Which one is that?"

Ms.MS: "Pyari dulhan"

MS. BD "Ha! How can you watch that? So very unrealistic".

Ms.MS: "what is unrealistic? Every thing is fine. Have you seen from the beginning?" Ms.GB: "Whatever you all say, good time pass, all of them. Can you imagine the evenings when the men are out to other cities and there is a lonely evening waiting for you. Surf, serial to serial and it is 11 o'clock, time to go to bed".

Ms.MS: "correct, it is good company. Not all of them are bad, like the one I see. Some real good messages are put across. For us it is fine, Village men and women, some section of urban ladies, who have had not much of education or exposure, out dated mother-in-laws, very traditional 'Do-not-want-to-change' families, such messages are eye openers. If it changes the thinking of even 10% of the viewers, it will be a great job done".

GMW: (She has to have the last word and give that valuable conclusion.) "True, when they are advocating widow remarriage, late marriages for both girls and boys, supporting women' s education, favouring child adoption, propogating the culture of working women, encouraging husbands to regularly be a part of household chores, these, if it happens, is a welcome change".

Ms. PS: "Listen, giving the correct perspective of caste, creed, religion, criticizing such issues when in the wrong, talking of one –child families, pushing people to exercise their right to vote, teaching them about consumer awareness and consumer rights etc it is commendable. Don't forget

Aamir khan's 'Satyamev Jayate'. Savdhan Ind.. timely warning. We must praise them for po.. such matters and bringing to the notice of the peop.. common man specially".

Ms. S& T: "Please be entertained, see and enjoy. Don't develop a headache thinking 'this is right, that is wrong'.

TH: "Yes, see the shimmering, embroidered, expensive saris, the blouses with their cuts (all of it cut off), those chunky antique jewellery, latest beads, danglers. The house décor, the curtains, the colour schemes, the furniture. Remember and if you like it, copy".

GMW: (A look of disdain on her face. Fortunately no one notices it). What with every one busy with their own thoughts. She thinks - Really, Some people cannot go beyond saris and jewels. What will happen to this country? (From the drawing room she has moved to the nation)

MS, BD: "Come on! Watching people get out of bed dressed as if they are back from a party. Not a hair out of place. The décor? Every house is a five star hotel. Looking at it, you will not copy, you will develop an inferiority complex. Saw the kitchen? No grease. no grime. A kitchen as huge as a restaurant with the latest Gadgets. The centre working platform with the freshest of fresh vegetables. What is cooked? Gajar halwa all the time.

By the way no problem of a cook. There is this nice 'Rasoiyya' always excellent and always in good mood. Even at midnight he will oblige you with 'garma garam bhajiyas'and cups of coffee, beaming from ear to ear. No servant problems either. They will shine everything to perfection, so much so that any dust particle 'aap dhoondte raha jaoge'.

Drawing rooms look more European than Indian. If Indian, then real ethnic, out of a housekeeping magazine.

The garden is complete with lush lawns, vibrant flowers. swimming pool, cane chairs and the inevitable bearer with tall glasses of chilled juice. Is this realistic? Is this correct?"

(Ms BD is quite spent after this long monologue. She falls back on her seat a little breathless. Surveys the room for the impact created. Others are mulling over what was said)

Ms.PS "BD please take it with a pinch of salt. Do you want to sit in the afternoons and watch dreary, dirty streets, poverty stricken houses, hungry families, drunken husband and a screaming wife. Sometimes watching things away from reality also helps. You can transport yourself to another kind of world and be happy. At least for some time you are not weighed down by problems, problems and problems. What is wrong with that? You can afford that much of indulgence, can't you?"

Ms BD:"They are the realities of life. Why are we afraid to face it? Why do we have to live in a surreal world? Only 'My entertainment, my pleasure'?

TH: Hearing the conversation and looking at the flushed faces makes a timely intervention. (Naturally! So much trouble to prepare everything from drink to dessert, arrange the house from drawing room to dining room and then some silly argument and all her efforts will go unnoticed. She cannot allow that. In fact won't allow it). She says, "Whatever it is. Daily soaps have become a necessary part of our existence. Like it or hate it, take it or throw it, it is here to stay".

Alltogether: Of course! Of course! Absolutely right. (all ladies and one consensus!)

"And the cars?" BD cannot forget. She has decided to continue the argument against the motion.

Others: "Cars?". "What cars?" "Who has bought a car?"

Ms BD: "In the serials. Every family is filthy rich. Nothing less than an Audi or a BMW. The poorest of them own a Honda city".

Point taken. MS decides, she needs to speak now, and then, BD is a good friend of hers. Sometimes they go out for shopping too. This is the right time to support her.

Ms MS: "Absolutely right. There is no place in the serials for a Nano or an Alto. This can be used as a social massage – 'save petrol'." Everybody looks at her praisingly. Ms. MS. leans back on the luxurious sofa importantly. MS feels, all the time we think of irrelevant matters. Think about saving fuel, clean environment, child labour. These kitty parties!!! She has forgotten, she had been one of the most enthusiastic founder members of these social get – together.

TH: "Come, Come, the phulkas will get cold. Talk while you have lunch. All proceed."

Ms. S and T: "How much have you made? Your table looks like the well laid out tables of our serials. Every thing looks delicious, served in the best of 'bone china'. Did you notice in the serials, any meal of the day is so elaborate. Truly, does it happen like that?"

After they settle back in the drawing room--

Ms. MS: "Have you all noticed? Every one, the men –all so handsome, all so impeccably dressed and the women— all so beautiful, all so elegantly turned out, Looks like average looks never existed in the world yaar. You develop an inferiority complex".

Ms. D: "Oh! I love that. Why should we see ordinary faces, weighty figures shabby dressing. Other characters are portrayed correctly. So have fun, watching the main characters who are 'great to look at'.

Ms GMW: "What I don't digest much is, either someone is all goody goody through out, the sati-savitris and Raja Harishchandra and Dharmveer Yudishthir and data Karna come to life or it is a bunch of mama Shakuni, Surpanakha, Kaikeyi ruling the roost. Characters don't change. Baddies keep hatching evil plots untiringly. Goodies keep being the sacrificial goat endlessly. There is no in between shades, it is either grey or white. The worst is that the bad ones don't even bat an eyelid to plan and execute someone. Is it right to screen such diabolic ideas? What if someone takes it seriously and turns out to be an imitator of such a gruesome episode".

TH: "I have planned some games. Let us have that. The discussion is going to be endless. Remember, serials are an integral part of our life now. We really cannot change anything. Serials will have drama about it, otherwise it will be boring and they will lose their viewership. Actually many people may be looking forward to such histrionics".

Ms.GB: "True. I would like to add one last thing. Invariably, in all serials you will find divorce and then re-marriages and re-re- marriages. The grooms are dashing, the brides are beauties. The boy is rich with a top job or a multimillion business in his pocket. Go to see in real life, to find one eligible groom is a herculean task". GMW: "But look at the other side of the coin. Why should someone live a life of misery because one marriage has turned sour. Everybody deserves a second lease of life".

Lunch over.

Ms. GB: "Come on we are making a mince meat of our TV channels. Actually, if serials are not your cup of tea, watch Sanjeev Kapoor's food channel, Animal Planet, National Geographic, DD National gives lovely old regional movies. You can watch cartoons and life is for laughs if you believe in 'laugh more to live more'. But, whatever you say they (TV soaps) are our company, watch them, if you disagree to something or you have a raised brow, You have salt at home—take it with a pinch of salt.? Poor joke I know. still it conveys, what I am trying to get at".

After 4 days. In the news paper:

'Due to disagreement between the government and channel operators all serials will not be shown for two days until further notice. Please bear with the inconvenience. They will come back at their earliest as soon as the issue is settled.'

Phone: Ms ST to GMW

Phone: Ms BD to Ms GB

Phone: Ms D to Ms PS …………

"What happened? Imagine the evenings. How disgusting! What will we do?

He (hubby) is not even at home to go out".

"What will my mother-in –law do? It is her life line. Poor thing that is her only time pass".

"My servant is dot on time for the 3:00 P.M serial, now God alone knows when maharani will arrive".

"Arre, while watching these serials, my daughter eats even brinjal". Now what? 48 hours to go ……….The countdown begins …….NOW.

Life's Small Memories

Train memory.

I was travelling to Jabalpur for my term holidays. For my company I had a mother, grand-mother and daughter trio. Educated, smart and friendly. Not only did they take care of me and looked after my comfort, they regularly plied me with idlis, murukkus, curd rice, taking pity on the hostel-starved-good- food-denied female.

At night I woke up amidst heated argument and a nasty fight between 'my trio' and another very sophisticated and important looking lady. The animosity next morning was so tangible that if looks could kill, everybody would be dead in the coupe.

I sat there like no-man's land between two countries' borders. Come Nagpur, my trio got ready to alight. There opponent questioned me "you are not with them?" Seeing my negative nod she retorted "I pity you young thing how did you survive them so long?"

The Grandmother looked belligerently and got down. The train whistled and chugged. Grandmother came back hurriedly to the window and told me "I pity you poor thing, how will you survive this lady for the rest of the journey"

Where else could 'TIT FOR TAT' come alive more than this.

Teacher's Memories:

* Apart from economics I also needed to take a subsidiary subject. So I taught history too. One question in the term paper was, "List down the achievements of Raja Ranjitsingh." One student began his answer like this "The achievements of Raja Ranjitsingh were: - 1) Raja Ranjitsingh died in the year 1839 AD.

* Nobody wanted to attend class. When the activity teacher announced that they needed students to act as soldiers everyone grabbed the opportunity and vanished leaving a handful of students in the classes. A week went by and the teacher announced that everybody had to pay Rs. 300 for the soldiers ensemble. Next day the classes were full again.